"Why don't you come over to my boat, Sundance, and we'll see what we can get cooking?" Tess said in a sultry, teasing voice.

He cupped her chin and gave her a searing look, then captured her mouth in a damp, deep kiss. She stepped away, her eyes gleaming playfully. "Follow me."

She backed across the gangplank to the *Lady*, blowing kisses at him. He vaulted across the distance and caught her in his arms just as she placed a foot on the detector panel.

The alarm buzzed shrilly. "I love it when I make women beep," he said.

She laughed, then sagged against him as his next kiss stole her laughter and tantalized her mouth.

The alarm buzzed again. "What is this, a game show?" he asked.

"Yes, and you've won the grand prize," she teased.

"What's my prize?"

Her breath was warm on his neck as she murmured, "Anything you want from me, Sundance."

She had no idea how much that offer might hurt her. . . .

WHAT ARE *LOVESWEPT* ROMANCES?

They are stories of true romance and touching emotion. We believe those two very important ingredients are constants in our highly sensual and very believable stories in the *LOVESWEPT* line. Our goal is to give you, the reader, stories of consistently high quality that may sometimes make you laugh, sometimes make you cry, but are always fresh and creative and contain many delightful surprises within their pages.

Most romance fans read an enormous number of books. Those they truly love, they keep. Others may be traded with friends and soon forgotten. We hope that each *LOVESWEPT* romance will be a treasure—a "keeper." We will always try to publish

LOVE STORIES YOU'LL NEVER FORGET
BY AUTHORS YOU'LL ALWAYS REMEMBER

The Editors

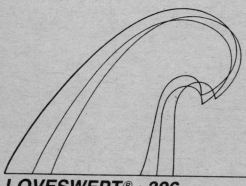

LOVESWEPT® • 326

Deborah Smith
The Cherokee Trilogy: Sundance and the Princess

BANTAM BOOKS
NEW YORK • TORONTO • LONDON • SYDNEY • AUCKLAND

To the Cherokee people,
who struggle so hard to
keep their heritage alive

SUNDANCE AND THE PRINCESS

A Bantam Book / May 1989

Published simultaneously in the United States and Canada

---

*Bantam Books are published by Bantam Books, a division
of Bantam Doubleday Dell Publishing Group, Inc. Its trademark, consisting of the words "Bantam Books" and the
portrayal of a rooster, is Registered in U.S. Patent and
Trademark Office and in other countries. Marca Registrada.
Bantam Books, 666 Fifth Avenue, New York, New York 10103.*

PRINTED IN THE UNITED STATES OF AMERICA

O   0 9 8 7 6 5 4 3 2 1

Prologue

A warm gust of April air swept over the new graves with deceptive innocence, carrying the fragrances of pine, oak, dogwood, and honeysuckle down to the magnificent spring-green valley below. The breeze lifted specks of red-tinted Georgia soil from the graves and dried the tiny spots where tears had fallen. The baked earth hinted that the summer of 1838 would be oppressively hot and tortured by drought.

To the young woman who placed white-blossomed dogwood boughs on the graves the air foretold more death, sorrow, and betrayal.

Because she was a Cherokee Indian, she whispered sacred formulas to guard the graves of her parents and sisters. Because she had graduated only a month earlier from the Philadelphia Presbyterian Academy for Young Ladies, she added prayers.

Because she was Katherine Blue Song, a proud girl of imposing character—but mostly because someone was watching—she didn't cry anymore.

The people of her tribe were being herded away from their homes like animals, in preparation for removal to the Oklahoma territory. Her family had resisted, much to the delight of the unscrupulous local militia. Now she was the only Blue Song who would have to leave the ancient homeland. Her family would remain here forever.

"I'm finished, Mr. Gallatin," she said in a tired but

formal tone, and straightened rigidly inside her plain black dress. "You may do the rest now."

The tall, rough-looking man stopped studying her with his perpetually intense gaze. Justis Gallatin touched a blunt gold spur to the side of his gray stallion. Then he tipped his wide-brimmed felt hat to her and ordered in a deep, drawling voice, "Back off, gal, so you won't get trampled."

She walked down the slope a few feet and stood staring into the distance, anger and grief burning inside her so terribly that she hardly saw the old blue-green mountains that were sacred to her people.

Gal. He was so crude, this chestnut-haired young man, with his unfashionable moustache and reputation for brawling, this white man who had been her father's partner until the government decreed that Cherokees could no longer mine gold.

Now he owned everything that had once been Blue Song property—the mine in Gold Ridge, the valley below, even the burned shells of the large frame house and barns on the hill behind her. Tears stinging her eyes, Katherine let her gaze drop to the distant creek where she had played as a child.

She tried to ignore the sound of his horse's hooves destroying the mounds of her family's graves.

He finally reined the big stallion to a halt and sat quietly watching her dignified profile. After a moment he offered, "None of those grave-robbin' bastards from town'll find 'em. You can count on it."

"Thank you."

Katherine was surprised by the gentleness in his voice, and she didn't trust it. She didn't trust him. He had money and power; he was white; the state of Georgia had given him and other white men the right to take everything that had belonged to her family, to her.

He stepped down from his horse, went to the small mare tethered to a nearby tree, and led her to Katherine. "Up you go, gal. It's not safe for you to stay here long."

Katherine faced him. "Of what concern is my safety to you, sir? You've done your duty."

He stared down at her with astonished gray-green

eyes that slowly narrowed. "I'm not gonna let Jesse Blue Song's daughter end up like the rest of the Cherokee women around here. If you don't know what the militia boys are doing to them, I'll tell you."

Katherine's knees went weak, and she almost choked on the pain in her throat. "Are you saying that my mother and sisters . . . ?"

She swayed and raised a hand to her mouth. Suddenly Justis Gallatin stepped close to her and took her in his arms. Her pride failed to keep her from leaning against him.

He cursed softly under his breath. "Forgive me, gal. No. That didn't happen to them."

She didn't believe him, but she was touched by his sympathetic lie. Her eyes shut, tears scalding her cheeks, she finally managed to say, "No one else cares. Why do you, Mr. Gallatin?"

He led her to a shady spot under a maple tree, and they sat down. He kept an arm around her, which offended her sense of propriety, but not enough to make her rebuke him. Her father had liked him and trusted him, which might mean that he was a good man.

But a blunt one. "I've got selfish reasons, gal . . . Miss Blue Song. You're a beautiful woman, a woman with education and culture. I want you for my wife."

Numbed and exhausted by grief, she gazed up at him in dull disbelief. "I won't marry just to have a roof over my head, sir. Besides, you *can't* marry an Indian." Sarcasm tinged her voice. "It would scandalize polite society—and your friends would call you a squaw man."

"Not up north. That's where I'm heading—gonna put some Gallatin gold into New York investments."

"Blue Song gold," she corrected. "Taken from Cherokee land. Stolen from people who were peaceful farmers and merchants."

"Your pa and I were in business together. There was no stealing on my part. I did everything I could to protect him and his, but I couldn't stop what happened. I didn't want to see the Cherokees driven off the land, and I fought many a white man over that difference of opinion." He paused. "Now. If you want to have a say in how the gold's spent, come with me. We don't have to get married until you get accustomed to me."

"How noble of you," she said drolly.

"Not the least bit. And I don't give a damn what polite society thinks of me. Never have. But I'll get you a chaperone—I'll hire you a wagonload of chaperones to keep your reputation up till we say the 'I do's.' How about that?"

"Mr. Gallatin, you're very presumptuous."

He shrugged. "You think on it, gal. You got nobody but me." Standing, he held out a hand and helped her to her feet. He swept an experienced, predatory gaze around the woods while one hand came to rest on the pearl-handled pistol tucked in his belt. "We best get back to town. I've killed my share of the trash roaming these woods. Like to avoid killing any today."

He looked down at her and spoke with another show of gentleness. "I'll walk off a little ways. You say your farewells. Say 'em good—you probably won't come back here."

She watched Justis Gallatin go to the horses, her mind spinning with the idea that this white invader thought he could have her for the asking; that she'd willingly become intimate with his moustache-draped mouth and lean, hard-looking body.

She didn't understand the strange sensation that thought created inside her, and some warning instinct told her she was better off not contemplating it. Slowly Katherine turned and faced the valley for the last time.

She ached with sorrow. This land of glorious forests, rivers, and rolling, blue-green mountains was part of her family, part of her blood.

As she grieved for all she'd lost she formed a silent, sacred promise to herself. Nothing must ever take this land away from her. There must come a day when the legacy of her family would live again here.

Katherine whispered a phrase in Cherokee. It meant more than a promise. It was a prophecy.

Someday.

One

The report was titled simply, "Gallatin, Tess—Profile of Suspect in Kara Diamond Disappearance." Above that title was stamped the national seal of Kara. Jeopard Surprise thought that the ornate red-and-silver seal was very pretentious for such a small Scandinavian monarchy.

It bolstered his suspicion that Olaf, Duke of Kara, was a pompous man, who would make a pompous ruling prince. Jeopard doubted the intelligence of anyone who'd pay twenty thousand dollars to get back a thirty-thousand-dollar diamond that had been stolen more than two decades before.

A small yellow note was stuck to the report's plastic cover. Jeopard eyed it, arched a blond brow at the message, and laid the report aside for a moment. With quick, efficient movements he punched numbers into the cordless telephone resting on his knee and waited for his brother's hearty hello.

When it came it had an echo, as if Kyle Surprise were hundreds of miles away, rather than in their office, five miles from Jeopard's apartment.

"Damn cordless phone," Kyle said solemnly.

"Stick your note elsewhere."

"Oh-ho, a direct hit to the Iceman's dignity."

"If I had any dignity, I'd tell people that I was an only child."

Kyle laughed at the barb, as usual. "That's cold, Iceman, cold. I thought you had a plane to catch for California."

"I'm going. Tell me what you meant by 'Don't scare her with your charm?' "

"The babe is used to young, fun-loving guys," Kyle shot back drolly. "Do your best to impersonate one."

And, chortling, he hung up in Jeopard's ear.

"Fun-loving" wasn't even in Jeopard's vocabulary. He raised a glass of brandy to a mouth made too grim by too many years of reading reports such as the one on Tess Gallatin.

He felt nothing but cold, professional curiosity about her. That lack of emotion had earned him harsh nicknames from enemies and respectful ones from friends over the years; it was the trait that made him so good at his work.

It was also the one trait that depressed the hell out of him.

He returned to reading the report. It contained the facts of her life in a concise, unequivocal list. Twenty-six years old. Residence: A sailboat, the *Swedish Lady*, Big Cove Marina, Long Beach, California. Widow of Royce Benedict, age sixty-two, jewel thief, died two years ago, cancer.

Father: Hank Gallatin, Cherokee Indian, Mercenary soldier. Mother: Ingrid Kellgren, Swedish, professional athlete. Both deceased.

Cherokee Indian? Jeopard scanned that information twice. She was half Indian? Well, at least that was different.

Occupation: Diamond broker. Education: Elementary and secondary—Smithfield Academy, London; college—UCLA, bachelor's degree in business administration.

Lifestyle/personality profile: Married Benedict when she was twenty; inherited his entire estate over objections of his two daughters; sexually promiscuous both before and after Benedict's death. Business associates rate her tough, manipulative. Approach with caution.

Jeopard almost smiled at that last note. While the brandy seared his throat, his eyes narrowed in a thoughtful squint.

Compared to the assignments he'd been given during his government career, her case was fluff. Even compared to the assignments he took now, as a civilian, her case was fluff. In effect, he was about to take his first vacation in ten years.

He flipped the last page of the report and studied a series of photographs. After he stared at them, mesmerized, for a long moment, he slung them and the report into a nearby trash can and downed his brandy in one painful swallow.

The cheap domestic rental car wasn't accustomed to Tess Gallatin's Grand Prix driving style. But then Tess Gallatin wasn't accustomed to cheap, domestic cars.

She steered the straining little automobile around a bend bordered by lovely, Victorian-era houses on one side and a tree-shaded college campus on the other. Picturesque little Gold Ridge, Georgia, backed by distant mountains, suddenly appeared before her like an obstacle course waiting to be negotiated.

It was so beautiful that it made her hurt inside with an odd wistfulness, as if she were returning to a home she'd never seen before. There were trees, lots of trees, and a brilliant blue sky untouched by smog.

Tess propped one olive-hued elbow out her open window and zoomed into the town square past a neatly preserved brick courthouse fronted by a dignified sign that read, "Welcome to Gold Ridge, Georgia, home of the first U.S. gold rush, 1829. Courthouse and gold museum open for tours."

In a musical British accent she murmured, "All right, Lawyer Brown, where are you?"

She checked her written directions, then peered at a tourist's mecca of quaint storefronts. Finally she spotted a glass door with "T. Lucas Brown, Attorney At Law" painted on it in gloriously ornate letters. T. Lucas Brown's door was sandwiched between a country café and a dulcimer shop. She swung the rental car into a parking spot so fast that when she braked, it made the tires squeal.

A minute later she was striding up a steep old staircase. At the top of it a ceiling fan hummed and clacked rhythmically over a reception area staffed by a Betty Davis clone wearing a white organdy dress.

Tess politely told her she had an appointment.

"Your cousins are already here," Betty informed her, puffing on a long cigarette. "You're late."

"How kind of you to remind me. I've never visited Georgia before. I left the Atlanta airport, took a right, and immediately got lost."

The receptionist scanned Tess's flowing turquoise dress and white fedora with a curious gaze. "Gawd, you're obviously from California."

Feeling more amused than annoyed, Tess cocked her head to one side and returned the appraisal. "You're obviously from Georgia."

Betty grinned, nodded, and punched an intercom line on her telephone. "The third one's here, boss."

A booming voice answered, "Dear Lord! A smorgasbord of beautiful women! Send her on in!"

Tess wondered what kind of lunacy she'd encountered as she went where Betty pointed. A rotund, black-bearded man threw a door open and exuberantly waved her inside. "Ms. Gallatin! Meet Ms. Gallatin and Ms. Gallatin!"

Her heart pounding, Tess stepped inside his office and gazed raptly at the two women seated in scroll-backed chairs by T. Lucas Brown's large desk. They stood, gazing back just as raptly.

The tall one, a lanky Amazon with shoulder-length chestnut hair and fair skin, was very businesslike, in a gray pin-striped outfit. The short one, a curvaceous Kewpie doll with an incredible mane of inky black hair and skin the color of dark honey, was very athletic, in jeans, running shoes, and a baggy T-shirt with a road-race logo.

The tall one smiled, came forward, and shook Tess's hand formally, but with genuine warmth. Her voice droll, she said, "I'm Erica. Born in Boston. My great-grandfather was Ross Gallatin, and that's about all I know concerning the Gallatin Cherokee blood. I own a construction company in Washington, D.C."

The short one grinned, came forward, and pumped Tess's hand merrily. "I'm Kat. Born in a circus trunk. My great-grandfather was Holt Gallatin, and I think he robbed banks for a living. I'm a nomad, although I have a dinky little apartment in Miami." She paused, thinking. "Oh. And I'm a professional wrestler."

After a stunned moment, Tess laughed. She'd known her cousins less than a minute, yet she already felt an affectionate kinship with them. "Tess Gallatin," she announced, and smiled at the double-take they did over her slight English accent. "Born in Sweden, raised in England and California. My great-grandfather was Silas Gallatin, and he owned a shipping business in San Francisco. I'm a diamond broker and I live on a sailboat in Long Beach, which is about an hour's drive south of Los Angeles."

"I'm a plain old country lawyer, and I'm fascinated by all three of y'all," T. Lucas Brown interjected, smiling at them. "Ladies, we have a will to read. Take your seats."

When they were all settled he looked at each of them, shaking his head in awe. "What a smorgasbord," he repeated. "None of you have met before?"

Tess traded apologetic looks with her relatives. They shook their heads almost in unison. T. Lucas chuckled. "Incredible. Do you know that you all share the same birthday?"

Tess turned toward Erica and Kat in amazement. "September twenty-seventh?" They nodded, as intrigued as she was. "But different years, I assume. I'm twenty-six years old."

"Thirty-three," Erica told her.

"Twenty-eight," Kat said.

"This has mystical implications," T. Lucas noted solemnly. "Which brings me to the reading of Dove Gallatin's will. Let's see, you share the same great-great grandparents, Justis and Katherine Gallatin—their sons were your great-grandfathers. That makes you cousins of some sort—third cousins, maybe. Who knows? Dove Gallatin was your great-aunt, Kat, and I'm too confused to figure out what that makes her in relation to Tess and Erica."

"My mother was Swedish. My father told me he was almost full-blooded Cherokee, but I know nothing about his family," Tess admitted. "Including Dove Gallatin."

"Same here," Kat added. "And I'm practically a full-blooded Injun."

"Ditto for me and the Gallatin Cherokee history," Erica said. "I'm only one-sixteenth Injun, umm, Cherokee. The Gallatins in my branch of the family didn't marry back into the tribe, the way Kat's and Tess's ancestors did."

T. Lucas Brown sighed heavily. "I hope Dove's bequest sparks y'all's interest in the family heritage. You can read her will if you want, but it's extremely simple. She left you two hundred acres of land north of Gold Ridge. The three of you are coowners."

Tess blinked in surprise. "Land?"

"Land that's been in the Gallatin Family for over a hundred and fifty years. It belonged to Justis and Katherine—probably belonged to her parents before that. Anyhow, Katherine's will stated that the land must pass down through the family. It went to her son, Holt Gallatin—Kat's great-grandfather—and then to Dove, his daughter. It can't be sold outside the family. It can, however, be leased.

"And you ladies will be happy to know that the Tri-State Mining Company has come to me with a lease offer for you. They suspect that there's enough low-grade industrial gold on your property to make a mining venture worthwhile. Y'all would get plenty of income to pay the property taxes and a small percentage of the mineral rights."

"Hooray!" Kat said. "Let's do it."

"Sounds terrific," Erica added.

Tess nodded. "I agree."

"Now, hold on, hold on. There's something else to consider." He reached into a desk drawer and retrieved a small cloth bag. Brown opened it and took out three large gold medallions.

Tess found herself gazing at them in open-mouthed wonder. They were nicked and dulled by years of handling, but the craftsmanship was superb. Each was a quarter-inch thick and at least three inches in diameter, and each had a small hole bored in it. The holes were worn as if by long use on a necklace.

Each bore a line of delicately molded symbols stamped in a circular pattern. The messages—if that was what they were—began at the outside perimeter of each medallion and wound to the center.

Brown flipped the medallions over. The strange symbols covered the other sides, as well. Attached to the hole in each medallion was a small white tag. Brown glanced at the tags, then handed the medallions out.

"It's absolutely magnificent," Tess whispered as she smoothed her fingertips over the strange gift. She glanced at her cousins and saw expressions of awe on their faces too.

"Each of you gets one," Brown told them. "Dove specified which of you gets which medallion. That's her handwriting on the tags."

Tess studied the bold, artistic script. "What do you know about Dove Gallatin?"

"Not much. She spent her entire life on the Cherokee reservation up in North Carolina; she was at least ninety when she died. She never married. She considered herself a psychic, I understand. I have no idea how she decided which of you gets which medallion. The symbols are different on each one. I believe they're Cherokee script."

"Hmmm, the tribe had an alphabet, correct?" Erica asked.

"Yes. Actually, it's called a syllabary. A remarkable achievement. Invented by a Cherokee named Sequoyah."

"Like the tree," Kat interjected vaguely, staring at her medallion.

"I believe the tree was named after *him*," Brown said with exasperation. "At any rate, ladies, I think it would behoove you three to track down some family history before you let a mining company tear up the Gallatin land. Supposedly the Cherokees buried their gold around here. These medallions may hold clues to something your ancestors left."

"Who made the medallions?" Tess asked.

"Don't know. Your great-great-grandmother Katherine, perhaps."

"Can you take us to see this land?" Kat asked.

"Sure, if everyone wants to."

Tess looked at Kat and Erica. They nodded eagerly.

Tess knew as soon as she saw the magnificent valley that she wanted to learn more about the people who had loved it. Erica and Kat stood silently beside her, their medallions clasped in their hands. T. Lucas Brown waited beside his Land Rover at the end of the old trail that was the outside world's sole access to this spot.

"I say we go back to our respective homes and do some research into our branches of the family," Erica suggested. "And we meet back here again in, say, a couple of months to decide about the mining lease."

"Good enough, Washington," Kat chimed. She gazed at Tess. "What d'ya say, California?"

Tess smiled. "If nothing else, I want to get to know you two better. Certainly."

She held out her right hand. Erica and Kat placed their right hands on top of it. Tess had the oddest notion that someone, somewhere, was watching with approval.

Whump.

Tess careened sideways on her lounge chair. The large, ostentatious yacht bullied its way into the berth beside her sailboat, bumped it again, and sent Tess sprawling to the deck on her hands and knees.

This was not how she wanted to spend her first day back from the Georgia trip.

"I'm not interested in a game of bumper pool!" she called to the person seated high above her on the yacht's navigation bridge. He grinned, waved, and steered frantically.

Tess staggered to her feet. Her *Swedish Lady* was forty feet long, big enough to have comfortable living space below deck and room for a patio table with a bright orange umbrella and four chairs above, but the yacht dwarfed it.

Muttering darkly, Tess shaded her sunglasses and squinted up, clutching the history book she'd gotten at the Long Beach Library. She'd been lost in the War of 1812, reliving Cherokee efforts to help Andrew Jackson fight off the Creek Indians, when the cumbersome hulk of a pleasure boat bumped the *Lady.*

She nearly fell down as the hulk slammed sideways into her boat again. "Slow down, you bloody maniac!" she yelled.

Against the sun she could make out only the silhouette of the man seated at the control console on the deck above her head. The yacht's bow plowed into the marina dock and bounced at least five feet backward.

Luckily for the yacht, the thick concrete dock was lined with a wood buffer.

Tess huffed in dismay. He was probably another weekend captain who'd rented a berth at the marina so that he could park his floating mansion and serve cocktails.

The interloper cut his engine off and stood up. Hmmm, at least this weekender had a nice build. Correction— he was wearing nothing but swim trunks, and he had a *fantastic* build, youthful but filled out.

When he raised his arms to ram both hands through his hair in disgust—the yacht was quickly sliding away from the dock—Tess was treated to an even more marvelous view of his body. He didn't look particularly tall, but he was so perfectly proportioned that she couldn't be certain. He gave "proportioned" a breathless new appeal.

And he was floating back out to sea.

Tess got up, stepped carefully around the *Lady's* mast, and went to the port rail. She cupped her hands around her mouth and called, "Come to the foredeck and throw me your lines!"

He looked down at her, a dark, intriguing form against the blue sky, his eyes covered by aviator-style sunglasses.

Tess waved toward the bow of his yacht with both hands. The movement opened the unbuttoned white shirt she wore over a black maillot. The newcomer pulled his sunglasses down an inch and studied her rakishly, smiling.

Oh, great, he was a pelican, she decided. That was the name she gave to men who watched her as if she were a tasty morsel floating on the water. Only problem was, this time she wanted to watch back.

"What's the foredeck?" he asked in a pleasantly deep voice.

The handsome idiot. "The front of the boat!" Tess ran to the bow of the *Lady*, crossed her gangplank to the dock, and went to the neighboring berth. Facing his monstrous boat, she yelled again, "Throw me your lines!"

"What's a nice girl like you doing in a place like this? I'll just bet that you like Capricorns, and I'm the sexiest Capricorn you're ever going to meet! Hey, babe, can I buy you a margarita?"

He was throwing her his lines.

Even if he *was* a dummy with more boat than sense, he was funny. Tess stared up at him for a moment, then broke into laughter. There hadn't been much to laugh about in the past several years, and she'd forgotten had good it felt.

"Captain, your lines won't hold!"

"That must be why I've had so much trouble docking lately."

He was smiling as he came down the staircase from the bridge, and despite herself Tess felt the effect of that smile. What she could see of his face seemed to be older than his youthful body, but that only made it more mesmerizing.

He trotted across his foredeck, and Tess fought to keep herself from gaping as she got a closer look at him. The sun glinted off tousled blond hair that was long and the rich color of wheat on top, short and dark gold around his ears.

The beautiful blond hair and his unforgettable, strong-jawed face reminded her of Robert Redford. Tess glanced up and down the busy Sunday-afternoon marina. Every woman within a radius of a hundred yards was staring at Captain Handsome.

Redford, definitely.

Moving with a fluid grace that stole her concentration, he lifted a heavy rope and carried it to the edge of the deck. A full thirty feet of bilge-green water separated him from the dock.

"Ahoy, me pretty," he yelled cheerfully. "Don't let me line catch you unawares."

It already has, she thought numbly. Around the marina she had a reputation as a recluse. One frustrated suitor had called her "the unmerry widow." So why was she staring up at Captain Blond as if she wanted to be his galley slave?

Tess clicked back to reality, stepped to one side, and watched him toss the heavy line with a coordinated strength that came from natural athletic ability. When it plopped on the dock she looped it around a cleat.

"You can pull yourself into place now, captain," she called.

"Great! The best place I can think of would be next to you! Come aboard! How about that margarita?"

Tess's illusions of Redford faded away. Oh, this pelican was charming, but she'd grown tired of being ogled by vain, immature men. California seemed to have an abundance of such types.

"Tow yourself in, captain, before someone clips you."

He clutched a chest covered in curly, dark-blond hair. "She ignores my witty invitation," he said, moaning dramatically. He staggered around, trying to look pitiful while he tugged at the bow rope and finally secured the yacht close to the dock.

"Thank you for your help, fair lady," he said in a raspy tone. "I just got this boat last week, and this is my first time docking it. You were very gentle with me. I'll never forget my first time with you."

Tess sighed. "You're welcome."

"I love useful women with English accents and beautiful bodies."

Tess grimaced at the tacky remark. She walked back aboard the *Lady* and picked her book up from the lounge chair. She decided it would be best to go downstairs and avoid Captain Tacky before he disappointed her more.

"Beautiful wench, don't leave!" he yelled plaintively as she started down the stairs to her cabin.

"You're on your own, cap."

"You saved me from washing out to sea! At least tell me your name, fair damsel!"

Tess pointed to her fawn-colored skin, then to the straight black hair that floated around her face and neck in a simple cut ornamented by softly structured bangs. "I'm hardly a *fair* damsel." The events in Gold Ridge tugged at her in a compelling way, and suddenly she added with pride, "I'm approximately half Cherokee Indian."

"I detest General Custer!" he called grandly.

"We didn't fight Custer. That was the Sioux."

"I root for the Indians in John Wayne movies."

"You're a credit to your boat, captain."

"I'm Jeopard Surprise. It's an old French name."

"Ever hear of the French and Indian Wars?"

He chuckled. "But the Indians were *allies* of the French in those wars!"

"Oh." Tess frowned. A good point. He was smarter than she'd expected. "See you around, captain."

"Your berth's registered to a Royce Benedict. Are you Mrs. Benedict?"

"Do you always investigate your neighbors?" she called.

"The information is in the marina's files for anyone who wants to know." He sighed dramatically. "I just don't like to park next to riffraff."

"Then you know without asking that I'm Tess Benedict and that my husband's deceased."

"I understand that your husband was a retired diamond broker—"

"And I'm neither riff nor raff. Don't play asinine games with me. Good day, cap'n."

With those cool words, Tess went downstairs and out of sight, where she closed the curtains, stretched out on her queen-sized bed, and tried to read her book.

Surprise. Jeopard Surprise. Who was he? What was he—aside from being a Redford imitator? And why did history suddenly seem so dull in comparison to current events?

* * *

Jeopard held a cold glass of water against his forehead as if it could ease his pain that way. Gone was the wisecracking facade, and in its place was his true persona—quiet, serious, brooding.

All his smiling at Tess Gallatin Benedict had given him a headache.

He picked up the phone beside his bed, called the shore operator, and had her patch him in to a Florida number.

"Kyle? Yeah, it's yours truly calling from Hell."

His brother's voice came back full of amusement. "It's supposed to be a fun job, Jep."

"It's a job."

"Well? Did you meet the infamous Mrs. Benedict?"

"With bells on. I acted so damned coy and cute that I nearly gave her sugar poisoning."

"Did she fall slobbering into your hairy arms?"

"Hardly. I screwed everything up. I'm no good at silly-ass chitchat. It was like flirting with Princess Di. Never joke with a woman who has a British accent. She saw through it, thought I was an idiot, and disappeared into the cabin of her sailboat—where she seems to be hibernating until I leave."

Kyle Surprise laughed uproariously until Jeopard cut him off with a terse string of obscenities. "Is she as beautiful as the pictures in the surveillance report?" Kyle finally managed to ask.

Jeopard hesitated for a moment, shut his eyes, and remembered long legs, high breasts, and cheekbones a model would envy. He remembered a noble, slightly hooked nose and alluring, deep-set eyes that revealed her Indian heritage.

He remembered exotic dark hair that wasn't quite black, and skin the color of a deep, golden tan. He remembered a melodic voice that sounded sweet even when she was annoyed.

He remembered that she was as sleek and expensive-looking as the silver Jaguar she kept in the marina parking lot.

"She'll do."

"Did she seem inclined to fit Olaf's description? A bed bunny? Ready to hop for every carrot that comes by?"

"She watched me as if she might entertain the notion, but she didn't exactly leap into my hutch. God, she's so young. I felt ancient."

"Chill out, gramps, you're only thirty-eight."

"I'm too old to play a male Mata Hari."

"This is a curse cast by all those poor women who trailed you over the years. For once, you have to be the chaser, not the chasee."

"Remind me to go back to my old career. Busting spies and terrorists was easier than playing private invesigator for the rich and famous."

There was dead silence on Kyle's end of the phone. Then finally, softly, "Not for me, bro. Not for me."

Jeopard winced. "Hey, kid, what did the doc say yesterday?"

"A few more silicone shots and I'll only resemble Frankenstein when I'm in *bright* light."

Jeopard felt a familiar ache of regret. Kyle had been badly hurt a year before during a mission in South America. A Russian agent had tossed him into a locked room with a pack of kill-trained dogs.

It had been the end of Kyle's enthusiasm for government work, and Jeopard had seen the end coming for himself as well. Millie, their youngster sister, had begged them both to give it up, but particularly Jeopard.

The years of danger, of losing friends and lovers to a voracious and deadly game, had taken a grim toll on him. Never one to mince words, Millie had told him that he was becoming something worse than the enemy he fought. He was becoming a machine.

And so he and Kyle had formed Surprise Import/Export, Inc., based in Fort Lauderdale, Florida. The innocent facade hid a quiet, lucrative trade in high-level investigative work. It could be dangerous at times, but compared to the old career, it was easy.

Or so it had been, until now. This fluffy Tess Benedict job was perfect for Kyle—charming, outgoing, fun-loving Kyle. Only, Kyle didn't think his face qualified him for such work anymore.

Jeopard hinted hopefully. "Even with scars, bro, you'd be better with this Benedict woman than I am."

Kyle's jaunty tone returned. "Oh, no, Jep. You're gonna learn to enjoy being coy and cute. I insist. Consider it a challenge."

"Maybe I can find out if she has the Kara diamond some other way."

"Oh?"

"Yeah. I'll threaten her with my Cary Grant routine. She'll have to tell me about the diamond or die laughing."

Kyle was still guffawing when Jeopard hung up the phone.

The antler charm. Tess was sitting on her cabin floor the next morning, surrounded by more history books, when she remembered it. Chastising herself for being senile at twenty-six, she hurried into the galley, went to a dining booth built into the wall, and knelt under the table.

She slid aside a specially designed panel and reached into the base of the booth, where a small safe was secured. A tiny light fixture, keyed to the opening of the panel, illuminated the safe's well-worn dial.

The safe had belonged to Royce for many years, and in its time had protected jewels worth millions of dollars. He had given it to her as a sentimental wedding present, and along with it the promise that he'd teach her everything he knew about diamonds.

Tess spun the dial quickly, and the door popped open. She reached in, pushed aside personal jewelry, personal papers, and a cloth bag containing a hundred thousand dollars' worth of uncut Brazilian diamonds—she had to deliver the diamonds to a wholesaler in Los Angeles the next week—and grasped a piece of deer antler the size of her thumb.

Her heart pounding with excitement, she quickly closed the safe and remained crouched under the table, studying the gift her father had given her not long before his death.

The amulet had been caressed by respectful fingers

until it was nearly white. It was made from the curving tip of a deer antler, and the blunt end was covered by a cap of gold topped by a tiny ring, so that the amulet could be worn on a chain.

Her father had told her that the amulet had come to him from his father, Benjamin Gallatin, a blacksmith on the Cherokee reservation in Oklahoma. It might have been made by Benjamin's father, Silas, the half-breed son of Katherine and Justis.

Enchanted, Tess studied the most important aspect of the amulet—the Cherokee symbols carved deeply into its surface. She went back to the cabin and retrieved the gold medallion she'd left laying among her books.

The symbols on the medallion were undoubtedly separated into words or phrases, and she squealed with delight when she saw that one of the phrases matched the symbols on the antler amulet.

The security buzzer sounded, meaning that someone had stepped on a detection panel hidden in the bow deck. Tess went aboveboard and met a tall teenage boy carrying an enormous arrangement of cut flowers in a ceramic base.

"Hiya, Tess," he said, peeking through the flowers. "Some guy called the shop and ordered these for ya. Mom said to tell ya she's thrilled to have a partner who gets guys to order two hundred dollars' worth of flowers."

"Brandt, good lord, who sent these?"

"Uh, uh . . ." He nodded toward a card stuck in the jungle of blossoms.

Tess opened it and read, "I'd like to bump into you again and throw you some more lines. How about coming aboard for that margarita? Jeopard."

She groaned at his determination. Dammit, why did this gorgeous, mature-looking man have the silly technique of a lounge lizard? If he'd bothered to ask anyone at the Marina more than superficial questions about her and her late husband, he'd know that her taste in men ran to serious, reserved types.

Tess squinted over at the yacht. There was no sign of the blond pelican, but she wondered if he was peeking through one of the curtained windows that ran along the yacht's starboard side. Pelicans were the type who peeked.

She patted Brandt's arm. "Come downstairs. I want you to take a message to Captain Pick-up. A *written* message—I wouldn't ask you to repeat my bad language."

Jeopard hated peeking out the yacht's window like some sort of socially backward nerd.

In the old days his agents had called him the Iceman, because of his emotionless facade and unbending dignity. The Iceman had confronted Third World dictators face to face without breaking into a sweat; he'd impressed the most brutal terrorists with his utterly cold demeanor; he'd traded urbane witticisms with powerful women and watched with objective pleasure while they turned into purring kittens.

And now he was hiding behind a curtain and cursing forcefully because the teenage delivery boy was still in Tess Benedict's cabin twenty minutes after delivering *his* flowers.

Jeopard ran a hand over his face and found himself tracing the deep laugh lines beside his eyes. Chagrined by his unaccustomed vanity, he jerked his hand away. Jeopard smiled sardonically.

If Mrs. Benedict was a cradle robber, then he might as well pack his gnarled old body back to Florida.

But there *was* hope—if he could impress her enough. After all, this was the self-serving woman who, at twenty, had married a wealthy man almost three times her own age.

It was definitely no love match, judging by the information Jeopard had received. She'd known from the beginning that Royce Benedict was dying of cancer. He'd taught her what he knew about diamonds and used his contacts to get her started as a respected broker.

Which was hilarious, considering that before his illness Benedict had been a jewel thief of international renown.

Jeopard sighed, hating the sordid business of prying into her life and wishing that his old cynicism would overwhelm him so that he wouldn't *care* whether Tess Benedict was a gold digger—or in this case, a diamond digger.

He peeked out the window again and saw the lanky, dark-haired teenager come back aboveboard. Tess Benedict followed, barefoot and wearing a loose white shorts set that didn't hide the lines of her A-class body.

The teenager wore only black running shorts and carried his Hawaiian-print shirt over one arm. The kid's hair was wet and looked as if it had been whirred in a blender—or by excited female hands.

What had she done—chase the kid into the shower? Was she *that* fond of jailbait? The kid couldn't be more than sixteen.

For the first time in years Jeopard felt human and vulnerable. He pinched the skin on his stomach, poked his thigh muscles, flexed his biceps, and went to study himself in a mirror.

"Sorry about the shower problem, Brandt."

Brandt rolled his eyes and shrugged. "No problem. At least it's fixed now."

"Poor kid. I owe you one. Want to drive the Jag to school next week?"

He whooped loudly. "All week? We get out for the summer on Friday. Until Friday?"

"Sure. If I need a car, I'll borrow my granddad's station wagon."

"You're great! You're really out there, Tess! You're fantastic!"

"I know." She smiled, patted his back, and walked with him to the dock. "Tell your mom I'll go over the books with her one day next week."

"Hey, what about the message for Captain Pick-up?"

Tess frowned. "Never mind. I'll blast him out of the water in person."

After Brandt left she stood beside Jeopard Surprise's yacht for nearly a minute, composing a firm speech. Her gaze drifted to the yacht's name, painted on both sides of the bow in black script edged in gold. She hadn't noticed it before.

Irresistible.

She shook her head in amused disgust. Tess climbed a wide gangplank to the bow deck and followed a canopied side deck toward the stern.

The yacht's windows were at knee level along the deck. Tess knelt down, one hand raised to tap on them. She really didn't mean to peer inside, but the curtains were thin.

Jeopard Surprise, wearing nothing but an air of concentration, stood in his luxurious bedroom admiring himself in a full-length mirror.

Two

She'd seen him in nothing but swim trunks the day before, but, oh, what a difference the loss of that simple covering made. His rapt scrutiny of himself confirmed her notion that he was vain. But in his case, vanity was justified.

His bedroom was small; after all, the yacht might be impressive, but it wasn't the *Love Boat.* So he was less than ten feet from her, and the sheer window curtains made him more tantalizing by screening him with gauzy white.

Tess remained by the window, her fist frozen in a tapping gesture, her insides dissolving into worrisome sensations of elemental attraction, her eyes riveted to the most undeniably beautiful male body she'd ever seen.

He wasn't beautiful in the sense of a sleek, boyish Greek statue; for one thing, he had a generous supply of hair on his chest, arms, and legs. He had the torso of a boxer—blocky and compact, not top-heavy with muscle. His upper body tapered only a little into his flanks, but there wasn't a spare ounce of flesh around his waist.

No, Jeopard Surprise's beauty came from a combination of muscle, grace, and virility that epitomized masculine charms. The virile part lay docile right now, but it was awesome, nonetheless. Like a sleeping lion, it looked ready to spring up majestically.

She doubted that he was more than six feet tall, but his legs were long, like a runner's, and they gave him the illusion of more height. They were wonderful legs, and the parts they adjoined, both front and back, were enough to make Tess sigh with plaintive admiration.

He might be preening in front of the mirror, but at least he was dignified about it, she admitted. He seemed very serious and intense.

Turning from side to side, he rubbed his hands up and down his stomach, stopping just short of the luxurious triangle of blond hair low on his belly. He nodded solemnly at himself, then twisted to look over his shoulder at his rump. He slapped it on one side as if he were testing for tone. Then he braced his legs apart and slipped a hand between them to poke his inner thighs.

Tess wasn't doing much breathing at the moment. She was thinking disastrous things.

This man had shown every sign of wanting to share his magnificent self with her.

Opportunities like this came along once in a lifetime.

What did she want—a meaningless affair or the kind of special romance she'd had with Royce? It was the question she'd debated over and over in the past two years as a steady parade of men tempted her loneliness.

The answer was always romance.

But wouldn't a meaningless affair with Captain Goodbody be a *little* romantic?

No—she wasn't emotionally equipped to have meaningless affairs. She thought about her feelings too much, put too much importance on commitment.

That was a result of her rootless lifestyle as a girl, when she had bounced between her grandparents' apartment in Stockholm, boarding school in England, and her father's beach house in California. She'd felt lost and lonely at times but had never doubted that her small, scattered family watched over her adoringly. That knowledge gave her security, a sort of intangible home, where she always lived.

And thus she knew the value of love, affection, and respect. They endured when nothing else did.

Tess groaned in dismay as Jeopard Surprise stretched languidly, every muscle taut and inviting. He stared at himself in the mirror, nodded again, then slapped both hands on his chest as if to say, *Good stuff.* He had obviously concluded that his appearance was acceptable.

She more than agreed.

She had to get a grip on herself. He might be married, she reasoned. Captain Goodbody might be any number of troublesome things.

He went to a bedside table, retrieved a copy of Robert Heinlein's science fiction classic, *Stranger in a Strange Land*, and lay down on the bed to read.

Tess began to tremble. She loved Heinlein. Any man who read him had at least a dash of intelligence and good taste.

She trembled also because the bed was right next to the window, and the view she'd had of Jeopard Surprise before was nothing compared to the view now.

If he wasn't married, maybe she could overlook the fact that he was a little bumbling and silly at times. . . .

She had to get off the *Irresistible* before she went overboard, she thought raggedly.

Tess leaped to her feet. Just as she did, she saw his head snap up sharply toward the windows. Ice water poured into her veins. Had he seen her?

She tiptoed along the side deck. Well, she rationalized, she was tiptoeing—quickly, to be sure—not running. Then she tripped on a cleat wound with rope, and had to acknowledge that a tiptoeing person wouldn't sprawl face forward with such a loud thud.

She heard his cabin door bang open.

Undignified escape maneuvers were now the only way to save herself. Tess scrambled to her feet and bolted. She'd hide aboard a friend's sailboat so that Jeopard Surprise wouldn't see her frantically scurrying onto her own.

If he came over later and asked whether she'd seen anyone suspicious aboard his yacht, she'd do the best inscrutable-Indian act since Tonto.

But it was too late. As she vaulted down the long gangplank she heard his running footsteps on the side deck and knew that he'd catch her.

Tess stepped onto the dock and halted. A dull, leaden feeling filled her stomach, while her face burned. She thought with a trace of grim humor that she probably gave new meaning to the term *redskin*.

He could now be heard running across the bow deck.

Tess turned around slowly, her chin tucked, and gazed up sheepishly. He came to a stop at the edge of the bow. Her mouth dropped open, and she gasped.

Gone was the bumbler who hadn't even been capable of steering his boat to the dock yesterday. His attitude was completely confident, as if he were used to chasing people—and catching them, as well. His face was set in lines that were neither angry nor cruel, simply businesslike. And that made him frightening. His eyes looked utterly cold.

Had this man ever smiled at her? Impossible. This man had nothing lighthearted inside him.

He was carrying a small cannon of a handgun, and the fact that he held it pointed in her direction didn't help her feelings. But he'd put on a robe, thank heavens—at least she wouldn't have to deal with his other weapons.

Tess realized suddenly that he hadn't seen enough to know that she was the intruder. She resisted an urge to point down the dock and yell, The guy went that-away!

Tess backed across the dock another couple of feet, clasping her hands protectively over her chest. Jeopard Surprise stared down at her, and a deep frown formed between his brows.

"It was only me," she called in a high, unnatural voice. *Please don't blast little old harmless me, captain. I swear I'll never peek at you again.*

After he scrutinized her for several seconds, the deadly look began to fade from his eyes. He blinked. His stance wavered, then relaxed, and he quickly lowered the gun.

"You? What the hell were you doing?"

The truth would not set her free. "Running. Falling down." She stared at the gun. "Fearing for my life."

He glanced at the frightening piece of artillery in his hand. A weary, self-rebuking expression crossed his face. "I apologize. Don't worry. I rarely shoot anyone I've sent flowers to."

"I'm very glad."

He remained still, studying the gun as if lost in thought. Tess watched with growing fascination as she realized that he was still rebuking himself for his reaction. Though frightened and puzzled, she felt drawn to him in an entirely new way.

Royce had often commented, with approval, that she loved to tease the limits of safety. It was evident in the way she drove a car, he said, and in the fact that she had married a jewel thief.

She hadn't believed Royce until that moment. Now she admitted that she liked a hint of danger, and the complex man above her offered not only that, but mystery.

He turned his attention back to her, squinted one eye, curved his mouth in a jaunty, knowing smile, and managed to look like the wise-cracking pelican from before. "When I put on a show, I like to have my audience *inside* the room."

"Don't get the wrong idea." Tess smoothed her hair back and cleared her throat. "I, umm, I came over to thank you for the flowers, and I . . . heard my boat's alarm system buzzing, so I had to hurry. . . ." She paused, frowning.

She was no good at such ridiculous lies. Tess lifted her chin and said defiantly, "Oh, hell, captain, I was coming to tell you where to shove your flowers. I accidentally looked into your bedroom window. After I enjoyed the show for a few seconds I decided to leave before you realized that you were being ogled. My only problem was that I decided too late. I do apologize, but you should buy thicker curtains."

With that she turned and marched back to the *Lady*.

Jeopard stared after her while his senses slowly returned to a lower level of alertness. Ogling him, she'd said. Enjoying the show.

He began to smile sincerely, and it was such a foreign thing that he didn't even notice.

Tess lay on her stomach in the middle of her queen-sized bed, crying without a sound, the antler amulet clasped in one hand, Dove Gallatin's medallion clasped in the other, a book open in front of her.

When the bow alarm buzzed, she brushed at her eyes hurriedly and said a small thanks for the fact that she didn't wear any makeup and therefore wasn't smearing any across her face.

A warm California night had descended, and the dock was a sultry place of shadows and pools of light from regularly spaced lamps along the water's edge. The other side of the dock abutted a thick concrete wall, and past it was a grassy lawn dotted with tall palms, beyond which was the marina parking lot.

Tess climbed the stairs from her cabin and found Jeopard Surprise standing on the bow, framed by a background of palms and suggestively shadowed by the dock lamps.

She halted at the top of the steps, her heart kicking into overdrive. He stood with one leg angled out, his hands shoved casually into the pockets of camel-colored trousers. He wore Docksiders and a white polo shirt.

"Well, Peeping Tess," he said solemnly, "the least you can do is walk over to the Zanzi Bar with me and have a nightcap."

She laughed, then applauded. "Bravo to your diplomacy and sense of humor."

He nodded, his attitude quiet and thoughtful. "I understand this place, the Zanzi Bar, is an up-scale hangout for the boating crowd around here."

"Yes." Tess tilted her head to one side and studied him curiously. "You seem different. Subdued. Did my ridiculous antics unnerve you?"

He chuckled ruefully. "I haven't met many women who'd have admitted what they were up to. It's unfair. My standard approach won't work on a woman as honest as you. I'll just have to be myself and hope for the best."

"Marvelous! I knew there was a likable, no-nonsense person behind that frivolous facade."

"Honesty," he grumbled. "I love it."

"I'm too honest, and it gets me in trouble sometimes. But I do like your new attitude."

"Good. Then let's make friends. Come along, Chero-kee princess. I'll buy you the firewater of your choice."

Tess didn't think twice about the invitation. She gestured toward her shorts. "Give me time to change into a different war bonnet."

"Should I alert the cavalry?"

She arched a brow. "After seeing you in action, I don't think you need help."

"In the bedroom, or chasing trespassers?"

Tess chuckled, felt her stomach drop languidly, and stifled a desire to answer, "Either." She pointed over her shoulder. "You may wait at my patio table, captain. I promise to hurry."

"I promise to wait."

She kept her word, and came back above deck to meet him less than ten minutes later. He sat at the table, slowly folding and unfolding a gum wrapper she'd left there, his head bowed in an attitude of deep thought.

Ah, yes, this side of Jeopard Surprise was more intriguing by the minute.

"I'm ready, Sundance. Stop thinking so hard."

He looked up, stood gracefully, and swept a slow gaze over her softly draped sundress of earth-tone shades. His assessment was bold enough to make her breasts tingle but debonair enough to avoid offense.

"Sundance?" he repeated.

"Surely people have told you that you could be Robert Redford's younger brother."

"Hmmm. I don't feel like a *younger* anything."

"How old are you?"

"Thirty-eight."

She hadn't yet gotten a close look at his face. During the events of the past two days he'd either been a few yards away from her, or wearing sunglasses, or camou-flaged by his bedroom curtains.

Even now the light was dim, making it difficult to study him. On impulse Tess reached for his hand and tugged. "Step forward, pops, and let me have a look at your wizened old face."

He smiled a little and did as she asked.

When she stood less than a foot from him in a soft

beam of light from the dock lamps, she could only stare up at him blankly, mesmerized. It was a distressful thing to have her mind go on vacation simply because his somber blue eyes were studying her back intently.

Tess murmured something without knowing what she said.

"Thank you," he answered. "I feel so much better."

She broke the spell by laughing softly and stepping back. But he wasn't through stunning her, and he stepped forward.

"If I put on some Ella Fitzgerald and we do this repeatedly, we'll be dancing," she quipped.

"I like your taste in singers. Okay, Pocahontas, where did you get those silver-blue eyes?"

"Daddy kidnapped a Swedish girl and took her off to his teepee. Pardon me, his wigwam. Cherokees didn't live in teepees." Tess gazed up at him in silence, trembling inside, her eyes riveted to his. "Yours are a darker shade of blue."

They were beautiful, intelligent eyes, she thought, and yet there was something shadowed about them, a coldness deep beneath the surface. But since the coldness wasn't directed toward her, she wouldn't worry about it yet.

He brushed a fingertip along the soft underside of her left eye, then her right.

Tess didn't know whether the boat was rocking or her equilibrium had just faltered. He'd touched her with incredible gentleness, using the same fingertip that had curled so expertly around the trigger of a deadly gun. The thought somehow reassured her that she had no reason to fear him, though others undoubtedly did.

She took a slow, reviving breath.

"Yes, my mother was Swedish. How's that for intriguing? A Swedish mother and a Cherokee father—I don't know whether to say *Yah?* or *How?*"

His mouth quirked up in delight. He seemed surprised that he found her so entertaining. After another second, he tilted his head back and laughed richly. Tess bit her lip and gazed at him with concern. If he kept this more mature charm going, she was in trouble.

"Damn, I haven't laughed like that—" He caught himself, smiled pensively at her, then frowned. He took her chin between his fingers and turned her face to one side and then the other, letting light fall directly on it. "Have you been crying?"

It was hard to remember what she'd been doing. "I was reading an account of the Trail of Tears. You know—when the U.S. government forced the Cherokees to leave the southeast and go to Oklahoma. It happened in 1838. Thousands of people died." She hesitated, then added softly, "My people."

He removed his hand slowly, his fingers almost caressing her as he did, and she had to concentrate to keep from leaning after them.

"I don't know a great deal about Cherokee history," he admitted.

"You probably know more than I do. I'm a novice Indian."

"Oh?"

"Come on, Sundance. I'll explain while we walk to the bar." She pointed to the medallion that lay between her breasts on a long gold chain. "I'll tell you about my inheritance."

"Hold my hand. I'm trembling from suspense."

Tess eyed his outstretched hand drolly. "White man speak with forked tongue."

"If you want to know about my tongue I can—"

"I'll hold your hand."

As she led him from the *Lady* she began explaining about Gold Ridge, Georgia, her remarkable cousins, and Dove Gallatin's mysterious intervention in their lives.

The Zanzi Bar, despite its too-cute name, was a cosy, intimate little place perched on the water's edge. As Jeopard sat facing Tess Benedict over their drinks, listening to her recount her Georgia adventure, he applied all his considerable skill to analyzing her.

Superficial impressions meant little in his business; he relied on a combination of instinct, observation, and cold, hard facts. His instincts told him that she was undoubtedly less shallow and self-serving than most people who were favored with money and unusual beauty. How much so, he didn't know yet.

His observations told him that she could be friendly, witty, tough, timid, and sentimental—the last only if she had been telling the truth about crying over a history book. Jeopard noted that she was perfectly at ease around the men who spoke to her in the bar. She seemed to know everyone. Men—and boys, he thought grimly, recalling the florist delivery boy incident.

She conversed with him in an unfaltering, intelligent way, as if she had no doubt that she was his equal in worldly experience. On that count she was woefully mistaken, but he admired her composure. He could believe that Royce Benedict had been attracted to her maturity as much as to her youth.

Her hairstyle and clothes spoke of chic tastes, but not vanity. They were uncomplicated, almost practical, yet very elegant in a European way. He had known European women who had incredible style even when wearing cut-off jeans and sloppy shirts. Tess Benedict had that kind of style—it was more a reflection of her personality than the amount she spent on fashion.

It was an honest and likeable style, one that seemed to extend to other aspects of her as well. Her voice, with its hint of England, was a melodic blend of cultured tones, and it could sound imperious or sweet.

He found it incredibly arousing, either way, but she didn't seem aware of that fact. If she wanted to seduce him, she wasn't consciously using her voice to do so. He decided that he liked that about her too.

So observation and instinct gave him inconclusive results. But the facts, as Jeopard had gotten them from the people who suspected her of harboring their diamond, said that she was a shrewd, manipulative young jet-setter who used people to get what she wanted.

And thus far, unfortuantely, she'd offered no concrete evidence to either support or deny the charge.

"So. That was my first foray into my Cherokee heritage," she finished, curving her hands around a tumbler of Scotch. "And I'm afraid that it's hooked me. I've been raising my consciousness lately."

And raising something of mine that I can't name that politely, Jeopard thought with a rueful smile.

"You think I'm whimsical, Sundance?"

"No. I admire your dedication. I haven't run across much dedication lately. Tell me more about yourself."

"I was born in Sweden. My mother died in a skiing accident when I was two. My father was an entirely wonderful man, and he loved me, but his work didn't permit him to raise a child alone. I grew up with my mother's parents, in Sweden, then went to boarding school in England. But I visited my father often, here in California." She paused, smiling at the memories. "The *Swedish Lady* was his boat. He left it to me." Her smile faded. "He died of a heart attack—oh, let's see— seven years ago. When I was nineteen."

"What kind of work did he do?"

The smile came back. "Have you ever heard of Sam Daggett?"

Jeopard chuckled. "He's second in my heart only to John McDonald's Travis McGee character. The Daggett books are classics."

"I'm glad you think so! My father wrote them!"

He looked at her incredulously. "Your father was J. H. Gant?"

"Uh-uh. Hank Gallatin. J. H. Gant was his pen name. And he lived quite a few of the stories he wrote about, I guarantee it. When he wasn't J. H. Gant, author, he was truly Sam Daggett, wanderer and adventurer. That's why I couldn't stay with him. He was always running off to exotic places to help some crony or other get out of trouble."

Jeopard stared at her with new fascination. Her father didn't sound like the mercenary who'd been described in the report.

Oh, hell, this case became more disturbing by the second. Sam Daggett, along with Travis McGee, had inspired his earliest—and most idealistic—dreams of adventure. Those dreams had culminated in a career in Navy Intelligence and eventually in more covert government work. His youthful fantasies were the only thing he still cherished about his career.

"You look as if I just handed you a Christmas present," she murmured.

"You did."

She took a sip of her drink. "Captain Sundance, I've been babbling about myself and I have yet to learn anything about you."

Professional wariness closed around him like an invisible cloak. "You know a lot. I'm a terrible sailor, I have a bedroom with, ahem, a full-length mirror, and I pack a large pistol for chasing women."

"We're talking about the Magnum .44, you mean," she teased.

Jeopard smiled wickedly. "That too." He couldn't help enjoying her. The fact that she had recognized the gun impressed him. Of course, J. H. Gant's daughter would know about such things automatically.

She covered her mouth and laughed in a way that was girlish without being the least bit shy. Her blue eyes held too much authority for that. "What do you do for a living that allows you to buy large pistols and cumbersome boats?"

He fed her his standard story about Surprise Import/Export in Fort Lauderdale. Her smile tightened, and she searched his eyes intently. Damn, he thought, she knew he was hiding something. Her intuition surprised him, made him feel oddly proud of her but also vulnerable.

"Jeopard, whatever you really do for a living, I hope it's not dishonorable."

He was glad that his control kept her from knowing how much she'd just shaken him.

"You say that because of the way I charged after you with a gun today?"

"Exactly. If your import/export business has anything to do with drugs, you can keep away from me. The farther, the better."

Inside he breathed a sigh of relief. Jeopard laughed with just the right amount of sincerity. "I'm clean, legal, and legit. I'll give you a business card tomorrow, and you can check me out."

She shook her head, smiled, and relaxed visibly.

He held up his right hand so that she could see the heavy gold insignia ring on it. "Naval Academy—Annapolis. The navy was my career until a few years ago. I was a SEAL. Do you know what that means?"

She nodded. "Special forces. Very elite. Also very tough."

"So you see where I get my gun-toting, Clint Eastwood habits?"

"All right." She nodded, satisfied, but after a moment of thought added wryly, "I guess SEALs don't learn how to handle yachts."

He chuckled. "It's not part of military training, no."

"So, importer/exporter, what are you doing so far from Florida?"

"I exported myself here for a two-week vacation."

"You had an, ahem, more experienced captain export your yacht, I hope."

"It's leased. I boarded it off the coast at Laguna Beach."

"Thank heavens you didn't have far to navigate before you rammed my poor *Lady*. The seafaring world wasn't threatened too badly."

"You're hurting my feelings."

"I suspect that few things hurt your feelings. However, I *do* apologize for maligning you."

He grasped his chest theatrically. "You'll have to do better than an apology. You'll have to have lunch with me tomorrow."

She clasped her hands on the table and looked at him formally, much like a schoolteacher addressing an errant boy, he thought.

"Captain Sundance, tell me the truth. Are you married?"

"Would anyone marry such a rotten docker? No."

"Ever?"

"No." He watched her try delicately to hide a frown. "Never fear, Tess, I have no desire to do your hair or redecorate your boat."

She gave him a rebuking look, but chuckled. "I wasn't asking for personal reasons."

"Oh? Are you a reporter for the *Marina Enquirer*?"

Her soft laughter crept into his bones and refused to leave.

"You silly lout. I can assume, then, that you're just another carefree playboy?"

"Playman," he corrected. "I passed 'boy' way back."

She laughed again. Jeopard took a slow swallow from his drink and wished like hell that she'd stop. It was not only the most seductive sound he'd ever heard; it was the sweetest. Instinct, observation, and cold, hard, facts began to give way to pure affection.

"I believe I *will* have lunch with you, Jeopard." She gazed at him happily.

Jeopard nodded, forcing himself to look pleased. He was too seasoned, too cynical, and too wise to let a job get to him. She was just a job, after all. If she had the Kara diamond, he'd get it from her. And when she realized his deception, she wouldn't have anything to laugh about for a long time.

Three

She couldn't wait to tell her grandparents about Jeopard Surprise.

At seven the next morning—bleary-eyed because she and Jeopard had sat at the Zanzi Bar talking until four—she parked the Jaguar in front of Viktoria and Karl Kellgren's Spanish-style duplex. The old, exclusive section of Long Beach where they lived was quiet and pretty; small homes and duplexes marched up the street beside tiny front yards exploding with colorful flowers and shrubs.

Karl and Viktoria met her at their door as usual, their arms wide, as if she didn't come every morning for breakfast.

They had followed her to Long Beach soon after Karl retired from a long and prestigious career in the Swedish parliament. Moving to America had been entirely their idea, but she adored them for doing it, and was glad that they were happy in the ultimate American playland that was California.

She didn't have a phone on the sailboat, so they kept a phone for her, a separate line with an answering machine. And because her relationship with them was so close, she didn't mind that they knew her business and social affairs.

So she sat with them in their bright little kitchen, eating a very Swedish breakfast of pancakes smeared with jelly, not tasting the food, her concentration devoted to telling them an enthusiastic but G-rated account of the intriguing man who'd become her neighbor at the marina.

After a half-hour of nonstop talking in fluent Swedish, Tess realized that their cheerful expressions had gone dark. "What's wrong?" she asked.

Her grandfather spoke first. "Why did you tell him so much about yourself so soon?"

Tess smiled drolly. "*Farfar*, only because the man asked. It could be that he likes me. I am likable, you know." She squeezed Karl's hand. "He's not the kind of man who feels comfortable talking about himself right away. That's the only reason he encouraged me to talk. It was innocent."

Viktoria nervously twisted the hem of the colorful apron she wore over a housedress. "But he wanted to know so much about your work and your family." She frowned. "You didn't tell him that you keep diamonds on your boat, did you?"

"No, of course not."

"And whatever you do, don't tell him about the blue. Don't wear it around him, either."

"That's right," Karl agreed.

Tess stared at her grandparents in disbelief. "You know I don't wear the blue. It's worth too much. What's going on with you worrywarts?"

"The diamond has been in the family for many years," Karl said sternly. "We wouldn't want it stolen."

"Good heavens!" She propped her chin in one hand and looked from Karl to Viktoria slowly. "Why are you worried now, but never before? Why didn't you worry when you gave the diamond to me? I was only eighteen. You didn't even worry when I married Royce, the ultimate diamond fancier."

"Royce was a friend of your father and mother's. He was an honorable man. We trusted him," Viktoria told her. "Since he's been gone you've ignored all the men who've tried to get close to you. Now, suddenly, this Surprise person takes advantage of your loneliness. . . ."

"*Farmor*, Royce has been gone for two years, and I'm lonely, I admit that. But Jeopard Surprise is very special. Besides, neither he nor anyone else knows that I have the blue."

"Just you be careful," Viktoria admonished, waving a finger.

"I could take it to the bank and put it—"

"No!" both Karl and Viktoria exclaimed.

"Don't show it to *anyone*," Karl said emphatically.

"It was your mother's. It should stay close to you," her grandmother added.

After a stunned moment, Tess sadly told herself that senility was making its first marks on her beloved grandparents.

"Good. I want to keep it close to me," she told them gently. "A thief would have to tear my boat apart to find the blue. I never leave it outside its special safe. Don't worry."

"I think we'll go down to the marina this morning and sit on your boat until we see this Surprise person," Karl announced.

Smiling benignly at their whimsical fears, Tess got up from the table and gave them each a kiss. "You guys do that. I have some phone calls to make, so I'll stay here." She paused, feeling mischievous, and added, "If he cranks his yacht's engine, run for your lives."

Sleepy-eyed, a cup of coffee in his hand, Jeopard glanced out his galley window a second time just to make certain that they were staring at the *Irresistible*.

Yep. Santa and Mrs. Claus were watching him from the deck of Tess's sailboat.

They both had graying blond hair. Santa wore a Panama hat and didn't have a beard, and their clothes were modern, but somehow the plump little red-cheeked pair evoked thoughts of elves and reindeer.

They sat at the umbrella-covered patio table, looking quite patient, as if they were just waiting for their binoculars to arrive.

They had to be the *morföräldrar*, the grandparents, Tess had mentioned the night before. Karl and Viktoria. The Iceman was under the surveillance of Swedish gnomes.

• • •

Tess sat on an overstuffed couch in her grandparents' living room, a note pad balanced on the pillow in her lap and a phone pressed to one ear. She was motionless except for the swift rising and falling of her chest.

"Gallatin, Gallatin," a drawling Oklahoma voice said on the other end of the line. "Checking the list, checking, hmmm, yes! Several Gallatins, starting with the census taken before the Civil War."

Tess felt like an explorer who'd just discovered a temple. "How could I find out more about them?"

"Awfully familiar name, Gallatin. Gallatin, let me see . . ."

Tess groaned silently as the woman rustled paper and mumbled.

"Wow! Wow! This might be very interesting!"

"What?"

"A biography of a half-Cherokee named Silas Gallatin!"

Tess threw the pillow in the air with glee.

Jeopard leaned back in his chair and cursed softly at the new wrinkle in what should have been a simple case. Cute little overprotective grandfolks didn't jibe with the background he'd been given about Tess Benedict. Of course, she could be a worthless piece of scum and still evoke love from her family—he'd seen that situation many times in his work.

Sure. Tess was scum. That was why he'd enjoyed every minute of the seven hours they'd sat talking at Zanzi Bar. That was why he'd resisted the urge to seduce her the night before, and had left her at her boat with no more than a quick kiss on the cheek and a joke about being too tired to aim for her mouth.

Sure. He didn't want her. He didn't want to breathe, either. The night before, he'd felt himself permanently slipping over the line that separated professional interest from personal interest.

Hell, maybe it didn't matter. He'd get the job done, regardless.

Where did she go every morning about seven? Work? No, she was dressed too casually to call on diamond wholesalers. A lover? The kid who'd delivered the flowers? Jeopard would rent a car and follow her the next day. It might be important.

Sure. Finding out if she had lovers was crucial to recovering the Kara diamond.

Suddenly he didn't feel like hanging around the marina to be gaped at by cute old people who made him feel dirty for deceiving their granddaughter.

He dressed in swim trunks and a T-shirt, then went outside and waved cheerfully at Karl and Viktoria. After a tentative moment, they waved back. He went to the bow and pulled the gangplank up, then detached all the lines.

Mastering this lousy dinosaur of a boat would keep him busy until she came back, he decided.

Karl's heavily accented voice assaulted Jeopard the minute he climbed to the navigation deck and sat down at the controls.

"Don't you dare bang her!" Karl called through cupped hands. The way he said it, it sounded like *Doan you dare vang er,* but the message still came across loud and ugly.

Up and down the busy marina, people raised their heads and listened.

Jeopard stared at Karl in grim amazement. The old bastard—yelling crude things about his granddaughter, in public.

"If you've got something to discuss with me, come on board," Jeopard called back in a stern tone.

"Don't you touch her! We don't trust you! Keep away!" the grandmother gnome yelled.

Jeopard had been warned many times in his work, usually by dangerous people, people who wanted him dead. He'd never flinched. He didn't now, but he wasn't certain how to handle this strange assault.

"You're embarrassing her, not me," he called back. "Now, stop it." He wanted to add, *I won't hurt her,* but he knew that was a lie. He wished that it weren't.

"Don't you bang der *Lady!* You keep away from her!" Karl jabbed a finger downward, at the boat.

Jeopard nearly choked. The boat. Don't bang the

boat. His jaw muscles hurt from straining, and all he could do was nod, salute, and go down to his cabin until he got himself under control.

Finally, after he'd wheezed his last laugh and wiped the tears from his eyes, he sat on the side of his bed and put his head in his hands. He'd try not to bang the boat, but he couldn't make any promises about Tess.

That realization made him feel absolutely, utterly heartless.

Tess was literally floating on air as she boarded the *Lady*. The two grinning, muscular college boys swung her between them on a seat made of their latched arms.

"You may put me down now, serfs," she ordered, laughing. They set her carefully atop the deck and bowed.

"Anything for you, my queen."

"Anything for a beer, my queen."

"You haven't changed a bit, serfs. Wait here. My castle is a mess, and much too small for a queen and two brawny rugby players." Smiling, Tess went to her cabin. When she came back she carried two bottles of beer and a thick leather scrapbook.

"Oooo, imported brew," one boy crooned.

"Would you expect the king's wife to drink domestic?" the other boy asked.

Tess handed them the beers and the scrapbook, brushing her fingers over the book in a loving good-bye as she did. They assured her that they'd be careful when they photocopied the prized collection of memorabilia and newspaper clippings from the two years Royce had coached a city-sponsored rugby team.

"No hurry about returning it," she called as they tromped away. "But be careful with it."

They blew her kisses out the window of their van as they left the marina parking lot.

Humming, Tess ran back to the cabin and quickly changed from her shorts outfit into sandals, white slacks, and a colorful tank top. She pulled her sleek, chocolate-colored hair back from her temples with white combs.

She went to a jewelry box where she kept her less-expensive items and got a pair of one-carat diamond studs for her ears. She put them on, then slipped a thousand-dollar Lady Rolex onto her wrist.

Next she fastened the antler amulet onto a slender gold chain and proudly hung it around her neck. When she checked her appearance in the mirror of her tiny bathroom, the amulet was all she noticed.

She couldn't wait to tell Jeopard what she'd learned on the telephone that morning.

When the buzzer sounded, Tess burst out of the cabin, looked up the stairwell to the deck, and waved cheerfully.

"Hey, Sundance, I heard that you encountered my grandparents. They said you took the yacht out and didn't hit my boat or the dock even once."

He nodded and tipped a finger to his dark sunglasses in jaunty salute. "I wouldn't dare, as long as they were here. You might say that I was *gnomed.*"

Tess laughed giddily as she locked the cabin door and began punching a numbered panel that activated her sophisticated security system. What a perfect day this was going to be!

She glanced up the stairs and sighed at the soul-stirring sight of him. This man probably didn't own a pair of jeans, she decided. He was wearing belted khaki trousers with a blue polo shirt.

But Tess liked his fashionable yet understated style. He had a sexy kind of elegance to him—like a blond James Bond, she thought.

"How are you today?" she called politely as she hit the last button on her security system.

"Ready to sweep you off your feet at lunch."

Tess laughed at his lighthearted tone.

Behind his sunglasses, Jeopard shut his eyes and wished he could do anything but spend the day with her. He'd witnessed her exuberant affection with the two college-boy types, and it only added to his troubled emotions.

Whether friends or lovers, they were obviously close to

her heart. He hoped they were lovers—he needed some harsh reality to restore his defenses.

She ran up the steps, looking delicious and cool, her white smile beautiful against the fawn hue of her skin. She grasped his hands and smiled at him until he couldn't help smiling back.

"I'm dragging you up to Los Angeles," she announced. "More specifically, to the library at the UCLA campus in Westwood."

"I'm game. What are we researching?"

She was trembling with excitement. Her voice hoarse, she told him, "I spent the whole morning talking to a woman at the Cherokee Cultural Center in Oklahoma. She told me about a biography written by a business associate of my great-grandfather Gallatin—the one who owned the shipping company in San Francisco."

She laughed with delight, threw her arms around Jeopard's neck, and hugged him hard. "And UCLA has a copy!"

Jeopard grimaced as the soft length of her body pressed against him and her delicate perfume filled his senses. Something tore apart inside him, and he was shaken by an all-encompassing desire simply to tell her the truth about his work and his mission there, then do his best to make her not care.

He forced himself to hug her in return, then step back casually, smiling, while his stomach twisted with fierce anguish.

It didn't matter whether she was hoarding a diamond stolen from one of the royal families to Europe, whether she might have married her husband simply to get that diamond and everything else he had, or whether she had a dozen lovers under the age of twenty-five.

Jeopard knew only that he'd been waiting all his life to feel her arms around him.

It took him more than an hour to do it, but he got his emotions under a semblance of control by the time he parked her silver Jaguar on a tree-lined boulevard near the UCLA campus.

"Incredible car," he told her. "Thanks for letting me drive your beloved."

"Considering my mood, I might have gotten another speeding ticket."

"Another?"

She nodded sheepishly. "My license was suspended last year. I got it back, and now I try to be more careful. Oh, I'm a perfectly safe driver. A perfectly safe, fast driver."

"Remind me to drive back."

She wanted to skip lunch in favor of heading straight for the library.

Jeopard did a Tonto voice and gestured sternly with one hand. "Great spirit say man and woman hunt food first." He leveled a hand over his eyes and scanned a bustling street lined with shops and restaurants. "Me see yuppie café. Come. We stalk nouvelle cuisine and white wine."

She laughed and let him tug her into a charming sidewalk restaurant. She also let him talk her into having two glasses of wine before her squid salad arrived, and by the time it came she was tempted to crawl onto the table and wave her own tentacles at him.

He asked polite questions about Royce, and she chattered at length about him, telling Jeopard how Royce had been delightfully British in a Peter O'Toole way, how he had been a crony of her father's, how he had come to California for her father's funeral and decided to stay.

Tess skimmed over Royce's work, as she always did when asked about it. He had been a diamond broker for many years, she told Jeopard, and was retired by the time they married. In a way, that was true. He sold diamonds.

He stole them, and then he sold them.

Jeopard's questions began to worry her, more so because she knew he'd tried to get her tipsy so that he could ask them. Tess smiled to herself. Jeopard thought she was an innocent, and his ploy sought to prove it.

But Royce had been an expert drinker, and he'd

taught her how to drink with business clients yet never give a secret, or a deal, away. The skill came in handy now.

"I must correct you on something," she told Jeopard with quiet confidence and composure. "You've referred to me as 'Mrs. Benedict' or 'Tess Benedict' several times. But I never took Royce's name. I've always remained Tess Gallatin."

"Any particular reason?"

She couldn't reveal that Royce had felt that it would be wise to distance her from his reputation as much as possible.

Tess shrugged lightly. "We felt that sharing a name was an antiquated custom."

His expression was inscrutable, but she sensed some challenge in the way his gaze held hers. "You seem more the old-fashioned type."

"Old-fashioned and demure? Hardly."

He smiled, but it didn't reach his eyes. "Good."

Tess knotted her hands together under the table. No wonder Jeopard considered her an innocent, she thought with self-rebuke. She'd run from the sight of him naked, she'd talked to him the previous night at the Zanzi Bar with childlike openness, and afterward, at her boat, she'd been too surprised to protest when he gave her a ridiculously chaste good-night kiss.

Tess got the perfect opportunity to demonstrate her sophistication before they left the restaurant. One of her regular customers, the owner of a large chain of jewelry stores, spotted her from the sidewalk.

Large, portly, and pin-striped, brandishing a thick cigar, Marvin Meyers invited himself to their table and started a brusque business discussion with her.

Tess leaned back in her chair, gave Marvin a cool, slit-eyed look, smiled, and showed her no-nonsense side. When they finished talking Marvin shook her hand with true respect and went on his way. She glanced at Jeopard hopefully and saw that her demonstration had been a success.

He was studying her with the somber, thoughtful gaze of a man who knew to take her seriously now.

"Well?" she asked, chuckling. "What do you think? Wish I'd been around to help the Indians who sold Manhattan. Offer us trinkets, hah! We don't need any crummy trinkets. Am I not a tough cookie?"

His blue eyes seemed to burn into her, and for a second she thought perhaps he was upset about something. Then he shook his head and smiled pleasantly.

"You're certainly convincing *me*," he told her.

She got tears in her eyes when a librarian handed her several envelopes of microfiche that contained Silas Gallatin's biography. She and Jeopard found a display machine on a nearly deserted floor of the library building and sat down at it side by side.

Tess stared at the envelopes as if they were sacred. "It doesn't look like a very long biography," she murmured in disappointment. "Maybe it's just about his shipping business. With a title like *Portrait of a Leader* it could be very impersonal."

"We won't know until we read it, Pocahontas."

She looked up at Jeopard, her eyes wetter than ever. "Forgive me for being so sentimental. It's just that I feel as if several important aspects of my life are converging all at once. As if nothing is ever going to be the same again."

Jeopard was very close to her. She saw another odd, unreadable emotion darken his eyes. The man was difficult to decipher, a fact she enjoyed.

"What aspects?" he asked gently.

Tess shivered inside at the effect of his voice. "Meeting my cousins, learning about my Indian heritage." She paused. "Meeting you."

A stillness dropped over him, making him seem poised on the edge of some monumental decision. His gaze went to her mouth. She felt his breath quicken against her face. If he leaned toward her just a few inches, he could kiss her.

But he didn't move.

Tess couldn't stand it. She tilted her head, parted her lips, and kissed him quickly on the mouth. Sensation sleeted through her as his lips responded with a skill that put a world of promise in the brief contact.

"We could get kicked out of the library for doing that," he joked in a gruff tone.

Tess struggled for enough air to speak. "At UCLA? We'd have to do something a lot more shocking."

"You've broken the rules before?"

Oh, no, another test of her sophistication. She *had* to reassure this worldly, experienced man. In a sultry tone she answered, "I went to school here right after I moved to California. I have a business degree."

"Which required lots of library time."

"Lots," she whispered.

He lifted a hand and stroked her cheek with his forefinger. "But you told me you married Royce not long after you decided to live in America. So you were married while you went to college."

Damn, I'm no good at these games! Tess thought in disgust. She'd forgotten what she'd told him about Royce. Now she could either admit that she'd never fooled around with any of her fellow students in the library—or elsewhere—or she could let Jeopard think she'd been an unfaithful wife.

Bluff. "I loved my husband, and I never did anything that would hurt him."

He stroked her lower lip. "You like keeping me in suspense."

"Life is more interesting that way." Breathing heavily, Tess managed to give him what she hoped was a wicked wink as she drew away and fumbled with the switch for the microfiche display.

From the corner of her eye she saw him settle back in his chair. She suspected that he was smiling patiently.

His tone was glib. "Speaking of suspense, Ms. Gallatin, your family history awaits us."

Thank goodness, she thought raggedly. History is safe. Her fingers trembling, Tess put the first sheet of microfiche into the machine and watched her great-grandfather's life reach out to her from the past.

• • •

Jeopard smiled grimly. Her predicament wasn't serious, and her comical distress reminded him of a distraught Lucy Ricardo.

Oh, Riiiicky. Waaaah! My great-grandmother ran a bor-dell-o.

"Take deep breaths. That's it. You're just hyperventilating. Let's sit down over here on the grass."

His arm around Tess's shoulders, Jeopard led her to a small park not far from where they'd left the car.

She clutched the thick handful of photocopied microfiche pages to her chest and kept clutching them even after he'd grasped her by the arms and helped her sit. He sat down beside her, tugged the manuscript away and laid it on the grass, then rubbed her neck gently.

"S-sorry," she managed to say. "We were in there for hours. Everything just hit me as we walked out into reality again. Great-grandmother was a madam. A full-blooded Cherokee hooker. I never suspected there could be such a thing. An Indian madam."

She bent her head into her hands and began to laugh.

Jeopard reminded her solemnly, "The writer only said that she ran a house of entertainment in the Oklahoma Territory not long after the Civil War. Maybe she had the historical equivalent of a video arcade."

Tess grasped his shirtfront and chortled loudly into his shoulder. "Pack-saddle Man."

Jeopard's throat contorted with restraint. She made it so easy to laugh. "Wide-Open-Spaces Invader."

When she squealed and thumped his chest with unrestrained mirth, he gave up. They both laughed wildly. She leaned against him and he put both arms around her. They rocked back and forth, gasping for breath.

Tess finally slumped in his embrace, wiping her eyes and reaching up to wipe his. They shared a droll look.

"I really think it's fascinating that my great-*farmor* was a madam," Tess admitted. "She may have done it out of desperation—she was only twenty-two when Silas took her away from the bordello. It's obvious that the Civil War devastated the Oklahoma Cherokees, and she probably had lost her family. Silas seemed like the kind of man who wouldn't care if he scandalized society, as long as he married the woman he loved. He sounds rather wonderful."

"See? No need to hyperventilate. And think of the other tidbits you picked up."

"It means a lot to me to know that the three gold medallions were willed to Silas and his brothers by their parents. It's a starting point."

"Katherine Blue Song. Now you know your great-great-grandmother's maiden name."

"Katlanicha Blue Song. Katherine was her white name," Tess reminded him. "I can't wait to call my cousin Kat. She's named after her—Katherine. I'm sure she'll want to know that her name has a fascinating background."

"We should fly up to San Francisco this week and find your great-great-grandparents' graves."

Tess grasped his hand excitedly. "I can't believe they spent their last years in California. Right in my home state! And I have to call my cousin Erica and tell her that Justis Gallatin was described as having 'burnt-red hair, like a chestnut horse.' That's the color of Erica's hair!"

She shut her eyes. "Oh, I don't mind hyperventilating over this. I feel like Sherlock Holmes after a successful case."

"Shouldn't that be Scalplock Holmes?"

Jeopard stroked her back and laughed with her again.

"Jep, I'm very glad you're sharing this with me."

He looked down at her laugh-flushed skin and happy blue eyes for several long seconds. She had unknowingly chosen the nickname used by his brother and sister, the only two people who loved him and kept him from losing his humanity. Maybe it was a good sign. "I'm glad too," he murmured.

He kissed her, kissed her hard, and felt light-headed when she kissed him back with a skill and passion that matched his own. He kept kissing her until a group of students strolled by and hooted at them cheerfully.

"We can't get kicked out of a park for smooching," Tess told him when he scowled after the group.

He looked at her, frowning. "I'd like an older audience, at least. How about dinner?"

She was trembling desperately in his embrace. "If we do this in a restaurant, we'll get kicked out for certain."

"Very funny. How about dinner aboard my yacht?"

"Can you cook?"

His heart was pounding in his chest. This was stupid, dangerous, and he was in way over his head. He pulled her more tightly against him. "Does it matter?"

She shut her eyes for a moment, and when she opened them, they were peaceful. "No. Not at all."

Four

They were quiet during the drive back to Long Beach, both caught up in the thoughtful, electric anticipation two people share when they've traded intimate secrets and expect to trade more.

Tess knew that she had, in effect, told Jeopard that she wanted to make love with him; the kiss and the simple words they'd exchanged were equivalent to a confession of desire.

Jeopard might be too practical to think of sex as *making love*, but she couldn't believe that sex was all he wanted from her. She knew she wanted much more than that from him.

Tess put a tape in the Jaguar's cassette deck, then rested her head against the soft white leather of the passenger seat and gazed out the window as if fascinated by the treeless brown hills and enormous concrete aqueducts that characterized southern California's landscape.

But every nerve was aware of the enigmatic, enthralling man who drove the Jaguar swiftly and with ease.

"Have you ever been a race-car driver?" she asked.

"Growing up I built and raced stock cars."

"Ah. I was right. I sensed that you know cars from the inside out."

He smiled his magnificent, controlled smile. "I know what goes where and how to keep it working."

"Ah. A skill for many occasions."

His chuckle rewarded her and made the bottom drop out of her stomach. Tess had never teased Royce suggestively, and it intrigued her that Jeopard Surprise made such teasing feel comfortable and not the last bit tawdry.

She knew it might be foolish to feel so sure of a man she'd just met, but she trusted her instincts. After all, she'd spent many hours with him in the past two days.

He'd told her all about his import/export business; he'd told her funny little human details about himself, like the fact that he'd once set his hair on fire in a high-school chemistry class and had a small burn scar on his scalp to prove it.

Most important, he'd told her about his younger brother, Kyle, who'd been injured by a neighbor's dog the year before; and about his sister, Millie, an ex-sheriff's deputy who was married to Brig McKay, the famous country-western singer.

Their mother had died when they were little, and their father had been a tough, demanding, career navy man, a chief petty officer who expected his children to take care of themselves.

Jeopard and his siblings had been shuttled from one naval base to another, and had learned to depend on one another rather than an ever-changing roster of friends.

Tess could tell that he loved his brother and sister; when he talked about them he revealed a pride and gentleness that warmed his eyes. It was the same gentleness that crept into his eyes at fleeting moments when he looked at her; she wasn't certain he knew it was there.

It was the promise of his gentleness more than anything else that drew her to him with such confidence.

Tess sighed and glanced at him. His close presence in the Jaguar made her belly tighten and goose bumps rise on her arms. Making love to the mysteries behind his shadowed blue eyes would be like uniting with a dark star. Her blood surged with erotic power at her ability to excite him; she craved more of the man who'd kissed her with desperate abandon.

Tess stopped looking at him, because the sensual

overload threatened her control. Her face already felt flushed and her eyelids heavy with desire. Her thoughts strayed to explicit images of his body intertwined with hers, his incredible mouth kissing her, his strong, seductive hands stroking her skin.

How could he sit there looking so unaffected by the energy she was sending his way?

"That's nice," he said of the ethereal instrumental music floating out of the tape player. "Who is it?"

"Suzanne Ciani. She composes New Age synthesizer music."

"Sounds like the surf. Makes me picture the ocean."

"Hmmm, yes. It's very soothing. I listen to it at night. It makes me dream about whales sometimes." She laughed softly.

He reached over and grasped her hand, as if the sound of her laughter had provoked him in some dramatic way. Tess groaned silently with pleasure, and waves of desire nearly dissolved her. She knew now that he wasn't unaffected by her; his skin was feverishly hot.

His voice caressed her. "Bring that tape with you to the yacht. We'll listen to it tonight."

Tess shivered and held his hand tightly. His warm fingertips stroked the cup of her palm. "I don't think it'll make me dream of whales."

"I hope you'll dream about me. I've got a little more to offer than a whale. I'm drier, for one thing."

She managed a low, delighted laugh that camouflaged her sudden urge to cry with gratitude. Royce had told her that she'd eventually find someone like this; a man closer to her own age who would inspire not only romance, but heady passion.

She couldn't wait to decipher his mysteries and learn everything about the man behind the cool, perfect mask.

Jeopard knew that she wanted him badly, and his intuition told him that there was something special in the wanting, something that made him unique. His age, he assumed grimly. She was accustomed to kids.

Bedding a full-grown man would seem like a novelty to her.

That thought, that he might be nothing more than a change of pace for her, didn't stop him from needing her more than he'd ever needed a woman in his life. Whatever her ugly truths—and he would learn them all before he was through—she was undeniably adorable.

For one thing, he couldn't resist her witty, provocative jokes. Lord, how many boys had lost their hearts while she perfected her seductive technique?

Nor could he resist her gentle sophistication. No matter how promiscuous she was, there was nothing coy or cynical about her intention to go to bed with him; just a sweet, silent admission in every touch, every look, and every inflection of her beautiful voice.

As they walked hand in hand down the dock toward his yacht, she smiled at people aboard neighboring boats, called to them by name, and swung his hand as if she and he were long-time lovers, not two people who'd known each other only a couple of days.

But she and he weren't strangers, Jeopard conceded silently. He doubted they'd ever been strangers, not even in the first moments when she stood below his bow as he docked the yacht, gazing up at him with amused disgust because of his tacky come-ons.

It was getting too easy to overlook every insinuation in the royal report from the Duke of Kara. What was the duke's idea of promiscuous, anyway? A few lovers— hell, Jeopard thought, he'd had more than a few lovers himself, starting in the tenth grade with Becky Partridge, a senior.

Jeopard didn't buy the idea that women ought to be less active than men; he'd known too many strong, intelligent women with the highest moral standards who also, incidentally, loved sex. Two years ago such a woman had died to save his life during an assignment in East Germany.

Jeopard was distracted from his brooding when a redheaded young man with the shoulders of a body builder and the tan of a George Hamilton hopped off a sailboat and swaggered his way down the dock toward them, grinning at Tess. He wore nothing but a bikini-cut piece of blue material masquerading as a decent swimsuit.

Tess smiled at him. "Good afternoon, Timothy."

"Hiya, gorgeous."

"Timothy, this is Jeopard Surprise. He's got the yacht next to me. Jeopard, this is Timothy Taylor. He works for the marina. I hire him to keep the *Lady*'s rigging shipshape."

Timothy shook Jeopard's hand, then winked at Tess and strolled on past.

"He needs to check his own rigging," Jeopard remarked. "He's a sail or two short. You ought to tell him that the kind of swimsuit he's wearing makes people wonder if he's trolling for boyfriends."

"Jeopard!" She looked at him in astonishment. "You don't have to worry about Timothy. He's extremely heterosexual."

He gazed down at her with a carefully neutral expression while disgust and anger grew inside him. He wasn't going to ask how she knew so much about the kid's sex life.

Hell, he could stand her having a lot of lovers, but he couldn't stand the realization that she might have several at once, and that he was only that evening's entertainment.

Suddenly he was furious at Tess, furious that he'd met his Waterloo in a pair of silver-blue eyes set in a face that belonged in a painter's portrait of a Cherokee princess. She'd reduced him to making petty, jealous comments about kids who shouldn't matter at all.

For the first time he understood exactly how much she had fouled up his work, his concentration, and his dignity, because he hadn't turned his emotions off.

Jeopard took a deep breath, focused on a cloud drifting over the sun, and cleared his conscience for what lay ahead.

Tess sat in Jeopard's lap, one arm draped around his neck, her free hand steering the yacht, the salty ocean wind streaking her hair back and whipping tears from her eyes.

He curled his arm more tightly around her waist, took another swallow from a glass of iced tea, and whenever she looked at him, demonstrated a heart-stopping combination of blond hair, sexy sunglasses, and a perfect masculine smile.

She was sublimely happy.

Finally she bent her head close to his ear and told him, "We've gone far enough from the marina! We don't want anyone to come tearing along the open sea and smash us!"

He nodded and cut the yacht's engine. The yacht began to slow. Tess took her hand off the wheel and circled Jeopard's neck with both arms. She was amazed that she could give him rational instructions about sailing.

The ocean made slapping sounds against the yacht, creating a provocative background of wet rhythms. Jeopard set his tea on a ledge by the control console and removed his sunglasses, then lifted his hand to her own sunglasses, huge lenses with tortoiseshell frames.

He carefully tugged them off her face, laid them beside his tea glass, then cupped her chin with his fingers.

"Well, here we are," he said pleasantly, as if it were an ordinary thing.

Tess's heart thudded roughly. "If you don't drop your anchor it will be *there we go*," she warned.

"Hmmm. Right." He led her downstairs to the main deck, kissed her lightly on the mouth, then went about anchoring the yacht.

The sun was setting behind him, and the sky framed him in deep shades of gold and magenta. Sunlight made a halo around his hair and outlined his body. He was still wearing his polo shirt and khaki trousers, but the outline couldn't have been more enticing had he been naked.

To test her theory, the next day she'd insist that he show her that view.

Tess watched him solemnly, her hands clasped behind her back, her knees weak. Privacy—that was what his suggestion to move the yacht had concerned. Neither of them had voiced such a thought, but it had lain between them, nonetheless.

It wouldn't have done to stay at the marina, where curious tourists sometimes climbed aboard the boats. She pictured a pair of explorers peeking into Jeopard's cabin that night. Tess didn't want to be part of anyone's vacation slides.

She felt a languid loosening between her thighs, and looked around with breathless amusement for a place to sit.

Why did you plop down on my deck, Tess?

Sorry, Sundance, you made my bones dissolve.

"I don't know what kind of show I'm putting on, but I'm glad you like it," he called.

Tess looked at him quickly, and realized that she was smiling.

"You drop anchor very well, Sundance."

"You should see how I cook."

"Is it a dramatic performance?"

"It's been known to draw applause."

Much like your other performances, I'll bet, she thought rakishly. She wondered about his past women. Oddly enough, he didn't act the part of a flirt, except with her. She didn't get the impression that he went around bedding just any woman who looked at him.

Good heavens, if he did that he'd have no time for eating or sleeping. Watching other women gape at Jeopard would have provoked her jealousy except that he never noticed their attention, much less returned it.

Her first impression about his vanity had been entirely wrong. He was the least vain person she'd ever known; she even sensed a certain embarrassment on his part, as if he wished he were more average looking.

A grand no way to that, my boy, she told him mentally.

He came toward her, pulling his blue polo shirt off as he did. He tossed it on the deck and spread his arms wide, eyes gleaming with invitation, the sunset making him look like an earthbound angel walking out of heaven. Her heart in her throat, Tess ran to him, and he put his arms around her snugly.

Tess looked up at him with devotion. His eyes became very serious, and he lifted her against him slightly, so that she stood on tiptoe.

"I think you wouldn't mind falling in love with me, Tess." He touched his lips to the tip of her nose and whispered hoarsely, "Even though we don't know each other very well. Tell me you're falling in love with me."

She gasped softly at his desire for this new and very important intimacy. Tess curled her fingers into his chest hair and bent her forehead to his shoulder while she took deep, shuddering breaths.

Finally she tilted her head back and looked at him. "I am. I don't care if we've just met. I've never felt anything like this before."

"Good." Again, he gave her a perfect, tender smile. "Not even for your husband?"

Tears rose in her eyes. Jeopard seemed to want to extract a commitment out of her in the most painful way possible. But then, she reasoned, it was only because it meant so much to him.

"I did love Royce," she murmured. "We had a beautiful relationship. But it was a mentor-student relationship in some ways—there was no way we could have a typical romance, not with the difference in our ages."

"And he was sick. Physically, he—"

"Jeopard." She grasped his shoulders firmly and looked up at him with pain shimmering in her eyes. "I know that you can do things for me that my husband was too ill to do very well. But I can't tell you that I didn't love or desire him, or that I wasn't happy with him."

"Sssh." He kissed her slowly, deepened the kiss with the erotic exploration of his tongue, then drew back and looked at her. "Say it again for me, Tess. That you're falling in love with me."

She swayed in his embrace, amazed at what had happened to her in the course of two days. "I'm falling in love with you," she whispered.

"There. That came to you as if you said it all the time, see?" He hugged her, nibbled her ear, and slid his hands down her colorful tank top to her white slacks.

He cupped her hips and rubbed slowly. Tess groaned

against his bare shoulder and licked his skin with the tip of her tongue. He was delicious, tasting of ocean wind and masculine musk combined with a fading trace of good cologne.

"Does love mean so much to you, Sundance?" She smiled into his skin.

"Yes." He curved his hands over her waist and drew them up and down her sides, touching her breasts with his thumbs each time. "I want to know everything about you. About your work, your past, about Royce. I want you to trust me and tell me everything."

"Oh, yes, yes," she answered, and put her arms tightly around his neck. "I feel that way about you too. Do you think you're falling in love with me, then?" She laughed sheepishly. "I'm just hinting for you to say so."

His hands tightened on her sides, his grip almost painful. "Oh, yes," he whispered. "I've been falling for you."

Tess looked up at him and lost what remained of her defenses. "I've wanted someone to share with for so long. I've been so lonely."

"Lonely?" He looked a little troubled. "Tess, I don't believe in sexual martyrdom. Please tell me you haven't been celibate since Royce died."

"Oh, of course not," she blurted out. Tess burned with embarrassment. She didn't want to appear foolish in Jeopard's worldly eyes. She managed a sly, teasing look and added, "Now, really, Mr. Surprise. Do I look that prim?"

He laughed, and for a moment she thought she heard a distressing undertone of sarcasm in it. But then he turned one of his mind-boggling smiles on her and she forgot everything except that she was gloriously happy.

"Are you hungry?" she whispered.

His blue eyes glittered with intensity. "The standard reply to that has to be, 'Not for food.' "

"I see." Her knees would turn to Swedish jelly any second now. She'd best take them below, where they could rest on Jeopard's bed. "Then we'll eat dinner later."

They went to his cabin, holding each other so close that their feet kept colliding and they nearly stumbled.

"I'm glad we're just going to make love," he teased in a gruff voice. "If we were about to dance, I'd be worried."

So he thought of it as making love. Tess was certain that he could hear her purring.

He opened his cabin door, and she stepped into the small, sumptuously furnished room. He closed the door behind them with a soft click. Tess stood in the shadowy room, her heart racing, listening to him move toward a tiny brass wall lamp.

There was another click, and gentle light turned the cabin into a cosy haven. "Ah, I remember it well," she said, pointing toward the gold-framed mirror on a door at one end of the cabin.

Jeopard stepped up close behind her and grasped her shoulders, pressing himself to her from shoulder to hips. His breath was hot against her neck. "Turnabout is fair play. I'd like to be the audience this time."

She barely recognized her own voice. "That can be arranged."

Tess walked away from him, stopped in front of the mirror, and smiled back over her shoulder. He stood very still, and she knew his gaze was riveted to her. Tess rebuked herself for the twinge of boarding-school-induced modesty that held her back for a second.

Royce had seen her naked, of course, but she'd never stripped for him.

"You're beautiful, Pocahontas," Jeopard said softly, as if encouraging her.

She relaxed then. Stripping was no more than shedding a few bothersome clothes. Tess removed her watch and laid it on a small table by the door. She caught her tank top with both hands and raised it over her head, then dropped it with a motion of one jaunty, gracefully curved arm.

He chuckled happily. "You've done this before."

Oh, every day, she thought wryly.

Tess ran her palms over the front of her delicate white bra. The chain bearing the antler amulet hung between her breasts; she cupped the amulet lovingly in her hand.

Her great-great-grandparents, Katlanicha Blue Song and Justis Gallatin, had found each other across two different worlds. Her great-grandfather, Silas Gallatin, had loved Genevieve Walking Light, the madam, despite her troubled past.

Tess didn't know anything about the relationship between her deceased grandfather and grandmother Gallatin from Oklahoma, but she did know that her father had loved her mother. It was obvious by the reverent and frequent way he had mentioned her over the years.

She come from a series of great loves, she thought with awe. And now she hoped she had found her own.

She took off the necklace and carefully placed it beside her watch. Then she latched her fingers into the front clasp of her bra and snapped it open. Tess raised her eyes and looked into the mirror, seeing her own flushed skin and gleaming eyes first, then Jeopard's face.

The coldness in it startled her so much that her hands rose to her mouth in alarm. He looked just as he had the other day when he was chasing an unknown intruder on his boat. He looked incapable of emotion.

"What is it?" she murmured. "What's wrong? Do I remind you of someone?"

He blinked in shock. Suddenly his expression was alive again. "My Lord, Tess, did I scare you?"

"Yes."

She cupped her hands over her exposed breasts and turned to face him. He came quickly to her and took her in his arms, cursing himself viciously under his breath.

"I'm sorry," he told her. He shook his head. "I don't blame you for being afraid of that face, Tess. But I swear it doesn't mean anything. It's an old habit from my military training. A bad habit. Don't let it unnerve you."

She chuckled ruefully, but felt herself relaxing because of his sincerity. "If all our troops could be trained to look at the enemy that way, we wouldn't need any other weapons."

He stroked her dark hair gently. "You're not my enemy, Tess."

"For a second, there, I wasn't sure."

His voice was practically an aphrodisiac. "Honey, that's the last way I'd ever feel about you."

Honey. With a low moan, Tess leaned against his chest. She laughed. "You might be descended from some Wild West Indian fighter. Those Indian-fighting genes could be hard to ignore."

"No, I'm descended from a Frenchman, remember? In fact, a French pirate who retired to Florida about 1835. He may have fought a few Seminole Indians, though, I admit."

"I forgive him," she said solemnly. "I'm sure the Cherokees fought a few Frenchmen along the way."

Jeopard's laugh was cut short when she raised her mouth to his and kissed him intimately. He shuddered, picked her up, and carried her to his bed.

Tess was overwhelmed by the quickness with which he undressed her; startled and aroused, she simply lay still and watched him, her breath fluttering in her chest. He undressed himself just as quickly and lay down on his side next to her.

"Tess," he whispered, drawing the backs of his fingers over her full, firm breasts. "You're fantastic."

Whimpering softly at his words, she raised a hand to stroke his chest. He intercepted it, kissed the palm, then pressed it down beside her on the bed.

"My treat," he murmured hoarsely. "Lay still and let me touch you."

She ached to run her hands over his body, but she was lost in such a daze of emotion and desire that she did as he told her.

He made it worth her while.

His expert touch mesmerized her. He squeezed her breasts rhythmically, raising the nipples so that his incredible mouth could do things to them that made her back arch. He smoothed his hand up and down her stomach, teasing her by almost but not quite reaching the apex of her thighs.

When she was panting and a fine mist of dusky pink colored her skin, he finally slid his fingers into the dark hair between her legs.

"You fit my hand perfectly," he murmured into her ear, then bent his head to nibble her neck.

The sound she made was almost a wail of pleasure. Tess grasped his forearm and stroked the corded muscles quickly, lightly, her touch conveying gratitude for the unforgettable sensations he gave her.

"Sssh, lay still now," he reminded her. He put her hand back on the bed.

"But I want to touch you so much," she murmured plaintively. Tess raised her head and tried to catch his mouth in a kiss.

He drew back, smiling tightly. She read the control in every line of his face. Oh, he was so dear, to give her pleasure this way when she felt the throbbing, hard evidence of his own need against her thigh.

"Now, honey, give me a chance," he said in a low, teasing tone. "I'm not an overanxious kid. I know the value of holding back."

Tess smiled quizzically at his odd words, then shut her eyes and sighed, the sound ragged. "Do with me what you want," she said in an airy, dramatic voice. "I'm yours."

He put his mouth against her quivering stomach and sucked for a moment. As she rose under him, crying out with delight, he murmured, "Good." He moved his magnificently tormenting mouth to another spot. "Mine."

As he placed slow, sucking kisses up her torso he reached for a shelf above the bed and retrieved something.

Tess made a small sound of protest when he stopped kissing her and edged away from her. He held up a small package that she recognized immediately.

He winked at her. "You won't have to worry about anything when you're with me. I believe in responsibility."

Tess felt too languid to move. On the way back to Long Beach she had hinted delicately that they needed to stop by a drugstore. He'd read her mind and said no, that early that morning he'd purchased the items she had in mind.

She had teased him to hide a touch of chagrin. "So you thought I'd fall right into your arms, Mr. Surprise?"

"I *hoped*," he answered in a sincere, quiet tone, and gave her an affectionate look that melted her worries.

Now she sighed again and gazed up at him with adoration. "You're perfect."

He said nothing, smiled mysteriously, and started to prepare himself.

Tess reached out. Her voice was hoarse with desire. "Please. Let me. Just let me do that much for you."

He hesitated, and she watched with dismay as his jaw tightened. "Jeopard? Do you not want me to touch you?"

Quickly his expression softened. "Honey, of course I do." He laughed low in his throat, but it was a strained sound.

Tess propped herself on one elbow. "What is it?" she said wistfully. "What's wrong."

He shook his head in mild rebuke. "This couldn't be the first time you've driven a man too close to the edge too soon."

"I . . . oh, I see."

Jeopard kissed her forehead. "Not to worry, Pocohontas. I won't let you down."

"Jep, I'm not worried about *that*. You just seem so intense. . . ."

He pressed her down on the bed and kissed her until she couldn't even think about talking anymore. By then he'd finished his preparations, and he slipped his hand between her legs again, stroking first one thigh, then the other.

"Spread your legs for me, Tess," he whispered.

She burrowed her head into the warm hollow of his shoulder and moaned. "Your wish is my command."

"That's it, Tess. You feel so hot and smooth."

He slid his fingers inside her, and Tess's world exploded in response. Everything she felt, everything she was, centered around the sweet destruction he brought to her restraint. She arched her hips and opened her mouth against his throat, calling his name.

Jeopard stroked her harder, adding ecstasy to ecstasy, and she squirmed desperately. Tess began to lick his throat with fervent movements of her tongue, like a wild, loving animal.

He shuddered from head to foot and immediately rolled on top of her. Tess slid her arms around his neck and cried out at the feel of his strong, hard body pressing her down into the mattress and angling between her thighs.

He cupped the back of her head to his shoulder and slid one muscular arm under her. Holding her almost fiercely, he nuzzled his face against her neck and thrust into her wetness with one smooth stroke.

Tess felt as if he had consumed her totally. She was so deeply wrapped in his embrace that she rocked with every quick, forceful movement he made.

His breath shattered against her neck, harsh and fast. She tried to turn her face to kiss him, but his grip kept her from it.

His embrace was overwhelming. It controlled her; it put her at his mercy. Something about his fierceness touched a small chord of distress inside her, and she kissed his shoulder tenderly, wishing that she understood what provoked him.

Her kiss drew a long shudder through him. He raised his head and gazed down at her with hooded, passion-filled eyes. Tess forgot everything except the raw sensation his gaze ignited in her body.

It amazed her—one look from those searing blue eyes and she rose under him like a magnet drawn to steel. She called his name again and dug her fingers into his lower back. *Jep. Oh, Jep.*

She shut her eyes. The blood rushing in her ears so harshly that she felt deaf, Tess dimly heard him groan and knew that he was watching the uninhibited expressions of pleasure on her face.

He was waiting for her pleasure to crest. She could only imagine what the wild contractions inside her must be doing to him. A second later she knew.

As she clung to him, trembling, he put his head on her shoulder and arched into her so deeply that he seemed to be entering her womb. Again and again he drove into her, then shuddered to a stop, holding her to him as if he'd never let go.

His release was so powerful and erotic that tears of awe came to her eyes. He drug his head up slowly, like a man just roused from a deep trance and still groggy. Both he and she were gasping for breath.

When Jeopard saw her glittering eyes he rested his forehead against hers and laid his hand against her cheek. His thumb brushed over the moisture on her lower lashes.

"Did I hurt you?" he asked.

"No. Oh, no." Tess stroked his head, raking her fingers through the thick blond hair. "You were wonderful." She hesitated, smiling while a big tear ran under his thumb. "You make me feel so incredibly *lucky*."

"This is just the beginning." He reached between their bodies and grasped himself as he withdrew from her. "Careful, now. There."

"Oh, don't go. Don't . . ."

But he was already off the bed. He went to the wall lamp and turned it off. The room was filled with streaks of white light from the rising moon.

Tess watched with bewilderment and sorrow as he moved through the magical light. Was the coldness so deeply ingrained in him that he couldn't bear to be treated tenderly?

"Back in a minute," he called softly. He went to the mirrored door and opened it. "Are you hungry?"

"Not at the moment."

"Me neither. Let's sleep awhile first. Get under the covers, Tess."

With that rather abrupt directive he disappeared into the bathroom and shut the door behind him. Tess watched bright light appear at the door's bottom and top edges. After a second she heard water running.

She wouldn't feel hurt, she told herself firmly. "Don't be a child, Tess," she whispered. He was terrific. What more could she want?

But a nagging inner voice answered, You wanted him to kiss you, not just press his face into your shoulder as if you weren't there. You wanted him to say your name. You wanted him to treat you like something more than a beautiful, convenient body.

And he hadn't.

Tess climbed wearily off the bed and stood in the moonlight, wondering how she should handle her concern. All right, she was a grown woman, and as such she couldn't be petty and oversensitive.

She'd give him time. He was the kind of man who didn't open up quickly. But then, he'd said he was falling in love with her. If that wasn't opening up, what was?

Tess frowned. He hadn't said he was falling in love, he'd said he was falling for her. But that was the same thing, wasn't it?

She groaned in frustration and jabbed her hands into her tousled hair. "Quit analyzing and get into bed, Tess."

She pulled back a thick bedspread richly colored in russet and bronze, then sheets that were some dark, indistinguishable color in the moonlight. Tess crawled under the covers and settled on the side next to the cabin wall. The yacht rocked gently, and she tried to let the movement lull her anxiety.

Regardless of her stoic words, disappointment and an odd feeling of loneliness lumped inside her stomach. Maybe he'd suggest that they go back to the marina so that she could go home to her own boat.

If he didn't want to spend the entire night with her, if he wanted her out of his bed after he finished with her body, she'd never forgive him. She'd never forgive herself for having such poor judgment.

He came out of the bathroom, shut the door, and crossed the room to her. "Comfortable?" he asked politely.

"Oh, yes."

She squinted in the shadows, trying to see what he was doing that made such odd metallic clicking sounds beside the bed. A tiny red light peeped into the darkness.

The ethereal music of her Suzanne Ciani tape filtered into the room.

"How's that, honey?" Jeopard asked as he slipped into bed beside her. "You said you liked to listen to it at night."

Tess swallowed hard to overcome the knot in her throat. *He'd remembered.* Oh, what a dope she was for getting so emotional over a few missed kisses, and such.

"Thank you," she managed to whisper.

Tess scooted over to him and curled herself to his

side, one arm across his chest, one leg over his thighs, her head couched comfortably on his shoulder. He inhaled deeply, affected by either her action or his own reaction. Tess decided to give him his privacy and not ask questions.

After a second he put his arms around her and rested his cheek on her head. She laughed gently.

"Jep, I'm not an oyster. You can't pop me out of my shell."

"Too tight?" His arms relaxed little.

"There. That's perfect, Sundance."

"Go to sleep, Pocahontas."

Tess relaxed inside his warm, possessive embrace. It might be more difficult to understand Jeopard Surprise than she'd originally thought, but she didn't doubt that he'd be worth the effort.

Jeopard was a light sleeper, a habit he'd acquired years before for personal safety, so he knew when Tess crept out of his bed near dawn and tiptoed through a door that led to the yacht's well-equipped kitchen.

He watched, frowning, when she came back carrying something, went into the bathroom, and shut the door behind herself. A few seconds later he heard the low hiss of water being run in his oversized bathtub. The water was running slowly, which made him think that she didn't want him to hear.

Jeopard plumped a pillow and sat up in bed with his hands latched behind his head, waiting. Okay, so maybe she was just the pristine type who didn't want to smell of sex when she woke up in the morning. He shut his eyes and winced.

He smelled her own feminine scents on his body, and he grew hard with just that little provocation.

They'd slept a few hours. He'd wakened to find her soft mouth on his, her hands touching him with a mixture of earthiness and delicacy that tore into his defenses. He'd satisfied her quickly, trying to keep his equilibrium when she writhed under him and called his name, as she had the first time.

Sometime after midnight he got up and fixed a platter of cheese and fruit. They ate in bed, sharing a bottle of wine.

Oh, Lord, all she'd had to do was get a little tipsy and tell him how happy she was to be with him. Affection and distrust had warred inside him so badly that he'd shoved the food off the bed and grabbed her like some sort of grouchy, lust-crazed bear.

He'd lain on his back and pulled her astride him in the hope that he could remain impassive while she took her pleasure, but it was useless to resist her.

As soon as she began to stroke his chest and stomach with feather-light fingers and rotate her hips atop him, he had arched into her wildly. Jeopard felt certain he wouldn't have reacted so strongly, had she not also whispered to him, her sweet voice telling him how gentle he was, how loving.

He'd been neither gentle nor loving with her, not by his usual standards with women. But either she liked sex that way or she forgave him, for some magnanimous reason.

He suspected, with heartsick self-disgust, that she forgave him.

The water stopped running. Jeopard heard muted sloshing as she got into the tub. Then there was only silence. He lay waiting for the sound of her washing, but it never came.

He gave her thirty minutes before curiosity and concern got the best of him. Jeopard rose from bed, pulled a dark blue robe around himself, and went to the bathroom door.

"Tess?"

No response.

He tested the door handle. It was unlocked. Jeopard eased the door open and looked inside.

She was asleep in the big ivory-colored tub, sitting crossways, her head lolling to one side on the tiled wall. Her arms rested on the back of the tub and her feet dangled over the side facing him.

Frowning, Jeopard moved quietly to the edge of the tub and halted, staring down at her. Her face was streaked with dried tears. A big container of table salt sat on the floor beside the tub.

Jeopard slowly sat down on the side of the tub and laid a hand on her leg. His voice was gruff. "Tess. Wake up."

Her eyes fluttered open, and she looked around blankly, startled. When she saw him she gasped. "I thought you were asleep!"

"I hurt you," he said grimly. "Dammit, Tess, why didn't you tell me?"

"Oh, no, no!" She became very officious, drawing her legs into the tub and straightening proudly, as if she weren't sitting there naked, soaking in saltwater. "You were fine!"

"Why were you crying?"

"I . . . oh, I'm very sentimental."

"About saltwater?"

She rubbed water on her cheeks and avoided his eyes. "I'm not hurt. Please go back to bed." She laughed softly. "This is between me and the bathtub."

He said a choice word of disgust aimed entirely at himself.

"Jeopard! Don't blame yourself! You were lovely!"

"I was brutal."

She looked at him in astonishment. "I didn't fake my pleasure at those times—and let me tell you something, Sundance, I'm not the type who'd enjoy it if you were 'brutal.' So calm yourself."

He studied her eyes for several seconds and concluded that she was sincere. "Then why?" He gestured toward the water.

"I'm a little tender, that's all."

His voice rose with exasperation. "Enough to cry because of it!" It occurred to him briefly that the famous Surprise aplomb was going up in smoke.

She looked distressed. "It's just that—well, you're rather large. I love it, but—"

"Thanks for the compliment, Tess, but I'm just average."

"Oh, no, I'd never call you *average*."

His patience was shot. Something was going on with her that he didn't understand in the least. He had a dire premonition that he'd made some terrible mistake.

Jeopard leaned over, braced his arms on either side

of her, and gave her the kind of look that had once reduced a Libyan terrorist to nervous chatter. She drew herself up even further, raised her chin, and gave him an imperious glare.

A Cherokee Katharine Hepburn, that was what he had there, he thought.

"Your fabled honesty, Ms. Gallatin," he ordered. "The truth."

Her mouth quivered at the reminder. She slumped a little and looked away. He could practically hear the wheels turning in her mind. She sighed deeply and looked up at him with great sorrow.

"I haven't made love in the two years since my husband died. And for a year before that, because he was too sick. I was never unfaithful to him, in the library at UCLA or anywhere else. I'm that awful thing you mentioned earlier, a sexual martyr."

She paused, her face full of regret. "So I wasn't quite in condition to go wild with you." Tess added wistfully, "But I'll be all right, if you'll give me a chance."

Jeopard felt as if his jaw might fall off. He closed his gaping mouth, frowned, and studied her face. He'd survived years of dangerous deceptions by learning the small physical signs that announced a person's lies.

Now he found the truth stamped unmistakably in her eyes. Dear Lord, her loving sweetness was no sham; there was nothing casual about her decision to make love to him. Yes, make love. That was what she'd called it, and he'd wanted to shake her for sugar-coating what she wanted from him.

Now he knew that she'd meant it.

Other questions tumbled through Jeopard's mind— had she inherited the blue diamond, not caring that it was stolen? Had she been Benedict's accomplice? Had she really taken his ill-gotten wealth over the protests of his daughters?

Those insinuations seemed more suspect than ever, but only time would tell. For now, he felt relief and hope sweep through him like a clean ocean breeze.

"You're looking at me so intently," she said, her face drawn with anxiety. "Please talk to me."

He leaned forward and kissed the frown line between

her eyes, which widened with surprise. "Tess," he said gently, "what a lady." Jeopard chuckled. "Clear up something for my feeble mind. Do you have any kind of romantic relationship with all those boys I've seen you with?"

Now her mouth opened in shock. "What boys?"

He told her quickly—the delivery boy, the boys who'd carried her to the boat, Timothy.

"Jeopard, what do you think I am, a cradle robber?" She raised a hand to her throat, as if the very thought were too bizarre to consider. "They're children! The delivery boy is my best friend's son, and the two college boys used to play rugby for a community team that Royce coached. And Timothy—he's dating a half-dozen girls under the age of eighteen!"

She looked at Jeopard as if he'd hinted that she liked to bay at the moon. "They're just babies!"

He resisted the urge to grasp her face between his hands and kiss her giddily. She wouldn't understand, at the moment.

"They're not babies, Tess, and a lot of women—"

"Good heavens! You thought . . . and now you're disappointed, you feel that you've gotten entangled with some sort of quaint Victorian . . ."

"Squaw talk too much."

He stood, grasped her gently by the arms, and helped her stand too. While she was still too surprised to react he swept her up and set her out of the tub. Then he grabbed a large towel and began drying her.

"What does this mean?" she demanded.

"It means I'm not disappointed that you have no love life. Or at least *had* no love life. Now you're going to have a helluva love life."

She wrestled the towel away from him and took his hands. Looking up into his eyes with shrewd scrutiny, she asked, "Why aren't you disappointed?"

"I thought I was one of several."

"Oh. And what do you want to be?"

"The only one."

That did it. Her anger puddled in the floor along with the bath water. Jeopard caught his breath at the new look of devotion on her face.

She gazed at him sheepishly. "I'll need a little vacation from bed. Just a day or two."

He raised her hands and kissed them. "You can sleep with me, can't you? And let me hug you, and kiss you, and you can ignore me when I get hard?"

She smiled as if he'd given her the most beautiful gift in the world. "Well, I don't know if I can manage that last part."

He chuckled. "I'll fight you away when you lose control."

"You really don't think I'm some prim oddity?"

"You're definitely a prim oddity," he answered, smiling and nodding. "But I love it that way."

The breath cascaded out of her, and she made a soft squeaking sound of relief.

Laughing, Jeopard finished drying her off. He carried her back to bed, tucked her close to his side, and got a lump in his throat when she kissed him good night. He curled his hand around hers.

"I should have told you the truth to begin with," she murmured sleepily.

"Every time, Pocahontas. Anything else you need to tell me?"

"No. I feel blissfully virtuous."

"Blissfully virtuous?" he teased.

"I'm allowed, now that you know my secret."

Jeopard shut his eyes and willed his mind to stop worrying about the future. Dammit, his new understanding of her life didn't make his job any easier, but he wasn't certain that he minded anymore.

He was falling in love with her, and he felt blissfully virtuous by association.

Five

Tess stopped reading out loud for a moment and looked at Jeopard with amused disgust. Resting in a white lounge chair on the yacht's upper deck, he reminded her of a lazy cougar. His eyes were shut, and even in relaxation his face was very private. She suspected that he was asleep.

He lay on his back with his hands behind his head, his feet crossed at the ankles. He wore nothing but a pair of low-slung white swim trunks. The sky behind him was as blue as his eyes.

If he'd had his eyes open.

"Sundance, are you listening?" she asked.

"Yes."

"Then why do you have your eyes shut?"

"That black temptation you call a swimsuit distracts me. And I enjoy meditating on the sound of your voice—makes me think of English gardens and tea with crumpets. It's hard to concentrate on Cherokee history."

"Oh." Smiling, she pulled her sunglasses down and eyed him rakishly. "I don't feel the least bit guilty for distracting a man who cheats at cards the way you did this morning."

"I got you flustered and you made a mistake. That's a legitimate tactic."

"Rubbing your bare toes over my thighs is not a legitimate tactic."

He laughed, the sound low and rich. Tess shifted on

her lounge chair, rearranged her history book on her knees, and bit her lip to keep from smiling at him helplessly.

As usual he made her feel languid and warm inside, like a flower just waiting for the sun to open it again. More important than that, he had won her trust and friendship completely.

He took pleasure in everything she did, even trivia such as the prim-and-proper way she brushed her teeth—a boarding-school regimen, she informed him. He wanted to know her favorite foods, her favorite books, her favorite *everything*. He was as fascinated with her as she was with him.

As a result, during the past few days the world had shrunk until only she and he were left in a cocoon filled with shared sensation and experience. Lord, she wasn't certain what she and Jeopard indulged in more— long conversations or making love. He was wonderful in both areas.

But Tess noted sadly that his view of the world was as dark as her view was light. That realization had become clear to her the previous night, when they'd discussed Paris. They'd both visited the city several times. Jeopard recalled only terrorist bombings and leftist politics; she recalled the restaurants, the architecture, and the art.

Tess sighed and shook her head. She was working on his cynical attitude and already making progress. Today he seemed almost jovial, and the guarded contentment in his face enchanted her. She smiled to herself. If she hadn't known him for an entire week— and thus gotten a bit accustomed to being enthralled— she would have thrown her history book down and pounced on him.

But she'd already done an embarrassing amount of pouncing since her recovery from the first night of, as she now referred to it, *excessive ecstasy.*

How could she help it? The man provoked her with tender kisses, affectionate smiles, and a husky way of saying her name. She couldn't believe she'd thought him cold and distant that first night.

"I was listening to you read," he assured her again. "Don't stop."

"Ahem. If you've been listening to me, sir, then summarize what I've just read."

He retaliated with a parrotlike recitation. "In 1838 the Cherokees who didn't want to be driven from the Sun Land, as they called their ancestral territory in the southeast, ran to the mountains of North Carolina and hid in caves there." He paused. "Where they developed a subculture of bat people."

"Be serious!"

Hearing the wistfulness in her voice, he stopped teasing. "Where they stayed until the federal government gave up trying to find them. A lot of them died from starvation. Those who survived helped form the eastern Cherokee band, and today they have a reservation in the same mountains where they took refuge a hundred and fifty years ago."

"Very good!"

"We should catch a quick flight up to San Francisco tomorrow and find your great-great-grandparents' graves."

"Would you mind?" she asked. "You must be bored by this personal-history quest of mine."

He rose, stretched, then came to her and tilted her chin up with a caressing hand. "No, I want to learn everything about you and your past."

Tess turned her face and kissed his palm. It didn't matter that he was learning a great deal more about her personal life than she was learning about his. He just needed time to open up.

"I'll make the arrangements," she murmured against the warm hollow of his hand.

"I've already made them."

Tess looked up at him quickly, a pleased smile on her face. He touched his fingers to her lips and winked at her.

People who have a good sense of humor usually have a good sense of humanity and of life, an aborigine shaman had once told Jeopard.

The man was a friend of Millie's husband, Brig McKay. In terms of outlook and personality Brig resembled a real-life Crocodile Dundee, and his Aussie friends were as eccentric as anything ever shown on a movie screen.

The shaman, enjoying an extended visit to Millie and Brig's home in Nashville, wore bib overalls and played the harmonica. He owned a grocery store in Brig's Australian hometown, Washaway Loo.

Not exactly a child of nature, Jeopard had thought.

But the shaman could predict rainstorms and tell how long the summer would last, and two weeks before Millie noticed any change in her body he'd informed her that she was going to have a baby.

When Jeopard met the shaman, the man had looked into his eyes for a long time and said, "You will be your own destruction."

That prediction had upset Jeopard more than he'd ever admitted. It came back to him even today, in the midst of a breezy, sun-soaked California afternoon while the ocean shushed peacefully outside the open windows of his cabin and sea gulls floated in the sky like small angels.

Jeopard knew the cause of his depression. He was going to make a phone call to Kyle while Tess took care of some minor chores aboard her boat. He felt sneaky, confused, and reluctant to tell Kyle anything ugly about Tess. All bad signs.

He was doing his job, doing it exactly as planned, and with any luck he'd get his hands on the Kara diamond in time for Olaf, pompous little ass and Duke of Kara, to unveil it for his subjects before his coronation ceremony. Olaf, who was the opposite of his popular aunt, the recently deceased Queen Isabella, apparently considered the diamond some sort of Holy Grail.

Olaf thought that getting the diamond back into the royal collection would improve his image. Jeopard smiled grimly. True. Everyone in Kara would then think of Olaf as a pompous little *ingenious* ass.

Jeopard tucked the phone into the crook of his neck and watched Tess come out of the *Lady*'s cabin. It was impossible to look at her without aching to hold her. Even thinking about her put him into hyper-arousal.

He felt like one of the boys he'd foolishly accused her of bedding.

But the worst pain came from his growing certainty that he wanted to spend the rest of his life getting to know her. He suddenly had so many things to talk about. Jeopard didn't understand why he'd never wanted to discuss them with anyone before, but a cruel little voice warned him that he'd lose something crucial about himself if he lost Tess.

She'd changed from her black swimsuit into a peach-colored sundress with a halter top. Her skirt swung fluidly around her bare legs as she moved about the sailboat, polishing bits of its trim with an old rag. Her dark hair fluttered like curtains about her face and neck.

She turned toward the *Irresistible* as if she felt his gaze, though Jeopard knew that she couldn't see into the dark interior of his cabin from where she stood. She smiled, raised a slender, honey-dark hand to her lips, and blew him a kiss.

Then she went back to her chores.

I could watch you for the rest of my life, Pocahontas.

His phone connection went through, and Kyle answered.

"Hey. Kyle. It's me, the brother you idolize."

Kyle, a colorful talker, began a detailed and bawdy analysis of Jeopard's faults. The point seemed to be that he'd expected another phone call long before that.

"How's it going with the seduction of the sea witch?" Kyle finally asked.

Distracted, Jeopard thought for a moment, then said, "She's having me to tea tomorrow." He cleared his throat. "Did you find out where the duke's people got their information on her?"

"They're vague. Kept saying they'd interviewed people who know her, but they wouldn't say who. But I double-checked the background on the diamond, and that's legit. It belonged to Queen Isabella, and it was stolen twenty years ago while she was visiting England.

"It was a hell of an embarrassment for the Brits, Jep. I talked to Edwards at Scotland Yard. He remembers the case. Royce Benedict was the prime suspect, but he had an alibi. They couldn't nail him, though they felt sure he was responsible."

Kyle laughed. "He was cocky. He'd stolen a million dollars in jewelry from Queen Isabella a few years before that. Served time in prison for it. The gems were recovered."

"What was this guy—the royal thief of Kara?"

"Sounds that way."

"Kyle, doesn't it strike you as odd that nobody wanted the Blue Princess back until now?"

"Look, the thing's not worth that much, as royal trinkets go. Apparently the Queen just wanted to forget the whole incident. After she died last year, Olaf decided somebody ought to settle the old score with Benedict. He's the vengeful type, from what I've learned."

"Good work, kid. I'll remember you at Christmas."

"Jep, Olaf's people want the diamond before the end of the week. The duke needs a public-relations victory real bad right now."

"Oh?"

"To put it simply, his future subjects think he's a dirt-sucking scum bag. There's a movement afoot in the parliament to kick him out and make the country a democracy."

"Fine. I'd like that."

"But they can't without rewriting their constitution. It says Kara remains a monarchy as long as there's a royal heir to the throne."

"I hope Olaf is the last of his species."

"He is—unless he finds a woman with no taste who wants to have his kids."

"I'll see what I can do."

"About finding a woman with no taste?"

"About getting the diamond, smart guy. If Tess has it. I don't think she does."

"You're getting softhearted or softheaded or both. Kiss Tess Benedict a few times for me," Kyle ordered cheerfully.

"You should get so lucky. And she uses her maiden name. It's Tess Gallatin, not Tess Benedict."

"She couldn't wait to forget Benedict, eh?"

Jeopard started to say something in her defense,

then frowned. He still didn't know what had motivated Tess to marry a dying man old enough to be her grandfather.

He glanced out the window and stiffened with concern. The two college boys—the ones from Royce's rugby team—stood on the dock talking to Tess. From their downcast expressions he knew they were upset, and Tess looked distressed too.

They handed her a bulky brown grocery sack. She cradled it in her arms and looked inside at the contents. Slowly she turned her face away, and Jeopard could tell from the boys' awkward, pleading looks that she must be crying.

"I have to go," Jeopard said abruptly. "I'll call back later."

He hung up the phone on Kyle's startled "But—"

Jeopard reached the dock in front of the *Lady* in time to hear one of the boys say, "I swear, Tess, the dog never did anything like this before."

She looked from him to Jeopard, her eyes glistening, her expression sorrowful. "Hi." She introduced them quickly, and the boys shook his hand. They squirmed, disgruntled to have anyone else see their misery.

Jeopard gazed at the bag, then up at Tess. "What's wrong?"

"There was an accident with my scrapbook." She gave the boys a sympathetic look. "It wasn't anyone's fault."

"My dog chewed it up," one of the boys explained.

"Tess, we know how much it meant to you," the other said plaintively.

"Guys, I understand. I really do. Forget it." Her jaw clenched and she blinked rapidly, trying to smile. "If Royce were here he'd say 'Why all the bloody nonsense over a heap of paper?' "

They smiled back wanly. When they left fifteen minutes later they were still apologizing.

Jeopard studied her carefully, torn between a desire to comfort and the need to interrogate her.

"Come on, we'll see what we can do," he murmured. Jeopard put an arm around her shoulders and they went aboard his yacht. Once in his cabin she sank down on the bed and spread out the remnants of the scrapbook. It had been thoroughly mauled.

Looking stricken, she gently arranged pieces of paper containing ripped photographs and newspaper articles. Jeopard sat down near her.

She looked up, her smoky blue eyes miserable. "I don't have much that belonged to Royce. He brought very few mementos with him when he moved here from England. His daughters received the rest—rightly so, of course." She touched the ruined scrapbook tenderly. "But that makes what I have more special."

"I didn't realize how much he meant to you."

She tilted her head to one side and studied him quizzically. "Why do you think I married him?"

Tess, I can forgive you for being tempted by a five-million-dollar inheritance.

"My vanity wants to believe that you were lonely and vulnerable after your father died. Royce represented emotional security."

She nodded. "At first. But he was hardly a father figure. He was quite a lady's man—a bit on the retired side in that respect, but a lady's man nonetheless." Tess paused. "Your vanity?"

Jeopard smiled devilishly. *Keep it light,* he warned himself. "I hate competition. Tell me you married him for his money."

She laughed. "Of course. Isn't that why all young women marry older men?"

Jeopard watched her gaze at the destroyed scrapbook again. Tears pooled in her eyes and slid down her cheeks. She wiped them away hurriedly.

"I'm an awful crybaby these days, I fear. Please don't think I'm always such a faucet."

Royce's money wasn't what made her cry over a whimsical scrapbook.

"You really loved Royce," Jeopard said simply.

"Yes."

He believed her, and another knot of worry unwound inside him. He was thrilled that she'd adored her husband. Sometime later he'd have to consider the irony of his feelings.

Jeopard paused, planning his next words. "How did

his grown daughters feel about having a stepmother younger than they were?"

"They thought their poor dad had gone bonkers, but they weren't surprised by it. He was never a conformist. I only met them once. They were extremely polite to me."

"And after Royce died?"

She smiled grimly. "They took their inheritance and bid me an extremely polite farewell. Don't call us, we'll call you."

"They didn't resent you?"

"Because of the inheritance? Hardly. Royce left everything to them."

Jeopard stared at her. He had just fallen off a cliff, but he was floating. He prayed that everything she'd told him was true. "How did you feel about that?"

"Oh, I knew he wouldn't leave me anything. He told me before we got married."

"But . . . honey, you took care of the man when he was dying. You suffered with him."

"Jep, I represented only four years in his life. Hardly anything in comparison to all of his family obligations. He helped me learn a marvelous profession, and I'm very comfortable financially because of that. Besides, I wasn't a hired nurse, I was his wife. I didn't resent having to take care of him toward the end."

Jeopard looked at her for so long that she shifted awkwardly and covered her face in mock embarrassment. She peeked through her fingers at him.

"Sundance, rest assured that I'm no saint. Stop looking at me that way."

He pulled her hands to him and kissed each of them. His lips against her warm, smooth skin, he asked gruffly, "Want some help trying to put Royce's scrapbook back together? I'm great with puzzles."

"Yes," she whispered, delighted.

Except in your case, he added silently. *I'm more lost than ever.*

The morning fog had just lifted when Jeopard guided their rental car through the steep San Francisco streets.

Tess hunched forward in the passenger seat, hands excitedly bending the sheaf of maps and written directions balanced on the knees of her aqua-colored chinos.

He glanced at her and smiled. She was as eager as a kid on the way to Disneyland, and he enjoyed her enthusiasm. In the past few days he'd absorbed her unsullied view of life until he almost felt lighthearted. It was easy to forget that he had work to do, or that he'd failed to get answers to his most important questions.

Did she have the Kara diamond? Had she been Royce's accomplice?

For today, he'd forget. He wanted to believe that this gentle, classy woman was everything innocent that he was not.

"Drive faster," she ordered, staring out the car window and impatiently tapping her white sandals on the floorboard.

"It's going to be at least an hour, Mario Andretti Gallatin. Sit back and take your gear off."

Her thirty-five-millimeter camera hung from a wide strap around her neck, indenting the abstract pastels on the chest of the fashionably huge white t-shirt she wore with a wide cloth belt. Also hanging around her neck were her gold medallion and her antler amulet.

Her chocolate-colored hair was pulled back in a French braid. Next to her he felt rather ordinary in a white golf shirt, dusky blue slacks, and Docksiders.

That was all right—in his business, it wasn't wise to draw attention with flamboyant clothes. He bought the best brands, and he had an eye for color, but he kept his style simple.

"You look like a Yuppie Indian," Jeopard said teasingly.

She flashed him a droll smile. "Silence, white eyes."

They left the city behind and headed north toward the wine country. In just over an hour they were deep into some of the most beautiful agricultural land in the world.

The rented sedan slipped through lush valleys filled with sheep grazing in emerald pastures and vineyards backed by tree-tufted mountains. The landscape was as picturesque as anything Jeopard had seen during several excursions in France, and when he rolled his window down he sighed at the heady, ripe scent of early summer greenery.

Tess made a husky sound of appreciation in her throat and slid over to him. She draped an arm around his shoulders and kissed his cheek. A poignant emotion filled Jeopard's chest.

"It's good to be alive," he said abruptly.

Tess laughed. "You sound as if you just realized that fact."

"Maybe."

She kissed his cheek again, and her voice was tender. "Jeopard, what have you done in your life that makes you so sad?"

Seen too many people die, he thought. "Spent too much time watching soap operas."

She chuckled but patted his shoulder kindly, her fingers caressing him through the material of his shirt. Her unquestioning, intuitive sympathy worried him a little. She sensed too much about him, which meant that one day soon she might find his dark side.

What would she think of her lover then?

"That's it!" she said suddenly, bouncing forward in the seat and pointing. "Glen Mary Road. To the winery!"

A minute later they were grinding down a two-lane gravel road between rolling hills striped with long rows of vine-covered redwood stakes.

In the distance an impressive stone mansion rose majestically amidst other stone buildings. The home was square and functional but enhanced by graceful turrets. Dense ivy covered the walls of the lower floor.

A sign at the driveway invited them to tour the Glen Mary vineyards, winery, and museum. Jeopard parked in a nearly deserted lot, and Tess bolted out before he removed the ignition key.

She waited for him impatiently, grasped his hand, and tugged him behind her while he jovially protested the indignity. They passed under a vine-covered arch, pushed open a mahogany door easily ten feet tall, and entered the mansion's foyer, a cool, marble-floored place decorated with Persian rugs and dark, heavy antiques.

An elderly woman in a tweed suit sat behind a desk.

She smiled up at them and said, "Welcome to Glen Mary. Ten dollars each, please. Here are your brochures. The upstairs is closed to the public because the current owner lives there. We hope you enjoy our gift shop and museum. The tour of the winery buildings begins in thirty minutes."

Tess did a good imitation of smiling nonchalantly during the woman's spiel, Jeopard thought.

"I'm Tess Gallatin, and I spoke to the manager about visiting an old cemetery on the property."

Thirty years fell away from the receptionist. She leaped up spryly. "Gallatin. Oh, my, yes. Mr. DeForest wants to meet you. He's the owner. He's so excited about your visit. If he'd gotten to talk to you himself . . ."

The woman motioned exuberantly toward a hallway. "Follow me. I'm Mrs. Johnson. I've worked here for years. You don't know what to expect, I can tell. I'm sure you'll be delighted. Oh, my!"

"Oh, my!" Tess exclaimed as the woman started into the main part of the house, waving for them to follow. She looked at Jeopard in shock. "She must know something about my family."

"Oh, my," Jeopard repeated dryly, smiling. He put a supportive hand under her elbow and propelled her forward.

"Here, look," Mrs. Johnson called, stopping at the oversized entrance to a large room. "Our museum."

Tess and Jeopard followed her into a softly lit, elegant room with tall ceilings and plush carpeting. Old photographs lined the walls; a restored grape press from the early 1800s sat on a shallow platform in the center of the room; various artifacts and memorabilia were displayed in glass cases. Mrs. Johnson hurried toward a corner and begin studying the photographs that hung there.

"I understood that there was a small Presbyterian church on the grounds back in the 1800s," Tess offered, "and my great-great-grandparents are buried in its cemetery."

"Would you like to see their photograph?"

"What?"

"Oh, my," Jeopard interjected on her behalf. But

even his cynical heart was thumping hard, and he wasn't sure who broke into a jog first, he or Tess.

Mrs. Johnson stood aside, beaming at Tess like a proud mother. Tess halted in front of a well-preserved Daguerreotype portrait inside a Plexiglas display box.

"Justis and Katherine Gallatin," Mrs. Johnson announced.

Tess made a soft keening sound and put her fingertips on the display box.

Jeopard gazed with fascination at the dignified couple in the portrait. Katlanicha Blue Song Gallatin's beauty was evident even in the stern, drab setting typical of old photographs. She sat in a high-backed chair, her hands folded in the lap of an incredible dress Scarlett O'Hara might have worn to a ball at Tara, had Scarlett had the coloring and features of a full-blooded Cherokee.

Her black hair was parted in the middle and pulled back into fat coils at the back of her neck, giving her a regal appearance. She was smiling slightly, and Jeopard thought her dark, compelling eyes held cheerful determination. He could imagine her issuing exasperated orders to her husband.

Justis Gallatin stood slightly behind her chair, lean and tall, one long leg bent slightly, one hand hooked into a pocket on his vest, the other hand draped over the chair's back so that the fingertips were twirled in a bit of ribbon on his wife's dress, as if he had been playing with it, teasing her, possibly.

His coat and trousers were formal and well cut, but his hair and moustache hinted that he cared for neither barbers nor fashion. He had craggy, handsome features scored with laugh lines around the eyes.

Judging by the challenging look in those eyes, Jeopard concluded that Gallatin also didn't care for photographers.

"They're magnificent," Tess whispered.

"This photograph was made in 1850," Mrs. Johnson told her. "In New York. It was sent to Mr. DeForest by one of their grandsons."

"Benjamin Gallatin!" Tess said, reading information on a placard at the base of the photograph. "This particular grandson of Justis and Katherine's was my grandfather! Do you know anything about him? He and Grandmother Gallatin were killed in a car accident when my father was a child, so I never learned much about them."

"Sorry," Mrs. Johnson said mournfully. "I wish I could tell you more."

"Oh, I'm so greedy! It's enough to see this photograph." Tess made a sniffling sound, then laughed at her own sentimentality. Jeopard slipped a handkerchief out of his trouser pocket and handed it to her.

"You can be proud of them," he told her gruffly. Did this romantic darling of a woman have *anything* of which to be ashamed? Dear God, he hoped not.

She continued reading the placard. Her voice became a low, incredulous rasp. "Justis and Katherine lived here? They started the Glen Mary winery?"

"We don't know a great deal about them," Mrs. Johnson told her, "but it's intriguing. The church you mentioned was built in 1840. We have sections from a diary the first pastor kept. He mentions that Katherine Gallatin came here in 1840 with her baby daughter, Mary. Just the two of them.

"And listen to this," Mrs. Johnson continued. "She was an Indian, but she'd been educated at a Presbyterian academy for women, in Philadelphia. The locals must have been impressed—they hired her, an Indian, to teach school in this area. That wasn't the kind of treatment most Indians received."

Tess pointed to the loving way Justis's hand rested on Katherine's shoulder. "But why would he let her leave him?"

"Maybe he didn't have a choice. We don't know. The first pastor moved away six months after her arrival here, and the next pastor didn't keep a diary. But Justis found her eventually, as you can see. They began this house and the winery. We think that they sold it in 1850. By then they had three sons. The children are listed in the church records."

"Silas, Ross, and Holt," Tess said softly. "But what happened to Mary?"

"She died when she was two years old."

Tess made a wistful, sympathetic sound.

"Glen Mary," Jeopard noted. "They must have named the estate in honor of her. That says a lot about their feelings."

"And they made certain that they'd be buried beside her, years later," Mrs. Johnson said reverently. Now she was becoming tearful too. She wiped her eyes. "I'll get Mr. DeForest. He'll show you the cemetery."

Sniffling, she left the room.

Jeopard idly patted his pocket, thinking that he should have stocked more handkerchiefs.

"Oh, Jep, this is incredible," Tess whispered.

He put his arms around her while she dabbed at her face.

"I wish I could get in touch with my cousins to talk about all this. They're both traveling or on vacation or something. Our lawyer in Georgia says he'll try to find them for me."

Jeopard stroked her hair, and she leaned against him, chuckling. "Did you ever expect to get involved with such a sentimental idiot as me?"

He kissed her forehead, then rested his cheek against her hair and held her tightly. "No, but I can't stop now. There's an old French custom that says once a man offers his handkerchief to a lady, he's pledged to protect her honor."

"Lovely balderdash. You made that up."

"No. As long as you keep my handkerchief, I'm yours."

She tucked the handkerchief into a pocket of her pants and gazed up at him adoringly. "Then I'm never giving it back," she whispered.

Jeopard managed a slight smile and ached from wishing that their future could be settled that easily.

Glen Mary's current owner was portly Reginald De-Forest. When he saw Tess, he clasped her shoulders with pudgy, bejeweled hands, and tears came to his eyes.

This was getting maudlin, Tess thought. She didn't mind.

"I'm such a history buff," he told her. "And I love

Indian history. You've been so oppressed. It makes me cry with righteous anger."

Tess thought for a moment. She'd never felt oppressed, personally. "Thank you," she offered politely. She looked up at Jeopard and knew that his solemn eyes hid amusement.

After she and Jeopard shared tea, tiny blueberry muffins, and Cherokee history with Reginald he guided them outdoors and gave them the keys to one of the estate's pickup trucks. Visiting family graves should be a private matter, he told Tess, and she kissed him on one bearded cheek.

Armed with Reginald's elaborate directions, Jeopard drove the truck down more than a mile of winding dirt road that led deep into the estate. It gradually entered a stand of trees.

"There," Tess directed. "There's the big oak tree and the old trail."

"Ah, you Indians. You make great scouts."

Jeopard turned the truck onto a path so narrow that tree branches slapped the windshield.

"There it is!" she exclaimed.

They entered a large, grassy clearing at the base of a gently sloping hill. Up the hill Tess saw gnarled old trees in the midst of much younger ones—there, as Reginald had described it, was the site of the old church.

At the bottom of the hill, canopied by ancient oaks scattered among the grave sites, lay a small cemetery.

"Let's go find them," Jeopard murmured.

They got out of the truck and walked among the old, weathered stones. Tess held Jeopard's hand tightly, anticipating the moment when she'd see her own last name spelled out across a gray monument.

Finally, there it was. In a separate plot surrounded by a low stone wall sat a dignified, steeplelike stone at least seven feet tall.

Gallatin was carved into it in simple, bold letters.

"Oh, Jep. Jep, I'm shaking."

"Does seeing your last name on the stone make you feel uncomfortable?"

"No. It makes me feel eternal."

A walkway led to the monument from an entrance

cut in the wall. Tess halted at the entrance, Jeopard close beside her. She felt as if her chest would burst from the sense that she'd connected with another something that was wonderful and important about herself.

Her Cherokee heritage and Jeopard. She'd found two beautiful new worlds.

"Hello," she said softly.

A bird broke into song somewhere on the hillside. A billowy summer cloud parted to let a streak of golden sunlight fall on the graves.

Jeopard's hand tightened around hers. "If I were a romantic, I'd say you've just been answered."

She turned to him, took his face between her hands, and kissed him tenderly. "You *are* a romantic."

He shrugged lightly, then released her hand and prodded her forward with a gentle touch in the curve of her back. "I'll wait here."

Tess moved down the short walkway, gazing raptly at the three smaller, beveled stones in front of the monument. Reginald DeForest had told her that the graveyard was overgrown when his family bought the estate in 1930; decades of rain and wind had scoured the stones until they were barely readable.

The DeForest family, history buffs all, had immediately had the cemetery cleaned up and the stones recarved. Tess read the inscriptions easily.

Our Cherished Daughter. She blesses the angels with her soul.

Wife, Beloved, Friend. All that my spirit holds, she has given.

Husband, Beloved, Friend. I shall take his soul to the Sun Land, for he is my home and my heart.

Tess read the inscriptions out loud, her hands cupped under her chin almost prayerfully. "They loved each other, Jep," she said over her shoulder. "I don't know why Katherine ran away from him and took their first child, but he found her and they stayed together the rest of their lives."

She pointed to Justis's stone. "The Sun Land. The name for the old southern homeland, remember? In Katherine's case, it meant Gold Ridge, Georgia."

"Maybe she thought she'd go back there one day, in spirit if nothing else," Jeopard said.

Tess knelt in front of a gravestone. "Katherine," she whispered. "You and Justis have three great-great-granddaughters." Tess took the gold medallion in her hand and drew her fingertips over its mysterious message. "And we'll make you proud."

All around her, birds sang.

Six

It was dark by the time they returned to Long Beach. Jeopard felt tired in a pleasant, satisfied way that made him relish a quiet evening with Tess even more than usual. The day had held a kind of magic, and he wanted it to continue.

He suspected that he was over the edge and hopelessly in love with her. The Iceman, who'd never let himself feel more than affection and respect for the women who shared his bed, who'd never had trouble walking away from a relationship, now understood what it meant to want someone beyond rational explanation.

Tess leaned companionably against him, her arm around his waist, as they walked toward the *Swedish Lady* and the *Irresistible*. The dock lamps made dramatic oblongs of light on the boats, and the night air curled inland with its bracing, briny scent. They seemed to be alone in the universe, and Jeopard liked it that way.

He drew her closer with an arm around her shoulders. "Tired, Pocahontas?" he murmured.

"Hmmm. And hungry. I have a baked chicken breast in my refrigerator. I can throw some vegetables around it and heat everything in the microwave. How about it?"

"I'll take your breast hot or cold."

They stopped by the *Lady*. She wound a hand in his shirtfront and looked up at him in wicked invitation.

Her voice was comically sultry. "You'll *always* get it hot, Sundance. Why don't you spend the night on my boat and we'll see what we can get cooking?"

Jeopard tugged at an imaginary tight collar and faked innocence. "I can't, ma'am. I don't have my toothbrush with me."

"Oh, I've got everything you need."

"I see." He cupped her chin and gave her a searing look, his mood now as sultry as her own.

Jeopard lowered his head and captured her mouth in a damp, deep kiss. She stepped away, her eyes gleaming playfully, her breath short. "Follow me."

She backed across the gangplank to the *Lady*, blowing kisses at him. He vaulted across the distance abruptly and caught her in his arms just a she placed a foot on the detector panel hidden in the bow.

The security alarm sent out a shrill buzz. "I love it when I make women beep," he whispered drolly.

She chortled, lost the laughter in his throat during their next kiss, and sagged against him as his tongue tantalized hers.

The alarm buzzed again. "What is this? A game show?" he demanded. "Is my time up?"

"No. You've won the grand prize."

Tess licked his lower lip, and his body's hard reaction told him that more privacy was a good idea. "What's the prize?"

Her breath was warm against his neck as she pressed a nibbling kiss there. "Anything you want from me, Sundance."

She had no idea how much that offer might hurt her.

Jeopard's passion lost its edge. He grasped her shoulders and looked down into her exotic eyes, with their gentle silver-blue glow.

Patience, he warned as he fought an urge simply to ask whether she'd been Royce Benedict's accomplice as well as his wife.

He was stalling, and he knew it. It would've been easy to wangle a night on her boat before now; he could have scrutinized the interior and calculated the most likely places to hide the kind of personal papers that would tell him where she kept the blue diamond. Then he could have searched the boat after she left to eat breakfast with her grandparents.

Jeopard winced inwardly. Every morning she left him to have breakfast with the gnomes. They wouldn't understand if their beloved granddaughter stopped visiting, and she didn't want to upset them with the truth. As a people the Swedes were sexually progressive, but as grandparents Karl and Viktoria were, well, grandparents.

Dammit, a woman who had gnomes for grandparents couldn't be a criminal. Which was an utterly ridiculous line of reasoning.

And one he intended to continue using.

The alarm buzzed again. Chuckling, she led him away from the security panel. Jeopard followed her down to her cabin door. When the stairwell hid them from public view he ran both hands up her thighs and caressed her rump.

"Stop, I can't remember the code number on my lock," she protested breathlessly, punching buttons.

"Thirty-six, twenty-four, thirty-four," he offered, drawing his hands up her sides and cupping her breasts to test his guessing.

"Close enough, and very flattering."

She pushed the door open, and they went inside. Tess flicked a switch that lit a brass lamp on a desk in one corner.

Jeopard had been inside the cabin several times, but only for brief periods while she gathered fresh clothes. Now he looked leisurely around, with more interest.

It was small, more cosy than practical, but undoubtedly comfortable. Her desk, bed frame, and shelves were made of some dark, rich wood, probably teak. The shelves were filled with books and stereo equipment. A jeweler's loupe lay on the desk beside a stack of business correspondence and a personal computer.

She was neat; her decorations were sparse, but appealing. A few framed paintings hung on the cabin walls; they were peaceful, flowing pastel abstracts. Jeopard decided that he'd enjoy meditating on that soothing artwork and lounging in her bed under its deep rose coverlet.

As long as Tess was lounging with him, he really didn't care about the surroundings too much.

"How about a glass of wine?" She went into her tiny galley and opened the door to a small refrigerator.

"Great. What can I do to help?"

"Lie on my bed and look handsome."

"The perfect job."

He kicked off his shoes and stretched out, shutting his eyes and inhaling her perfume from the bed pillows. A small air-conditioner hummed in the window on the port side. Thick white curtains on the starboard window assured complete privacy. The boat was definitely outfitted for marina living.

And hiding stolen diamonds?

No. He believed in gnomes and their granddaughters.

"Well, how was it?" Tess murmured into his ear.

Jeopard lay with his head on her bare shoulder. She arched a little as he drew his hand up and down her torso, pausing to rub her dark, taut nipples each time. Making love had never been a spiritual experience until he met Tess.

He crooked his hand over her hip and pulled her closer to his satiated body, then angled one leg between her thighs. "An eleven on a scale of one to ten. I don't know which I like best, when you seduce me or I seduce you. I'll seduce you in a minute so we can compare results."

Tess chuckled a little as she stroked his shoulders. "Actually, I was asking about dinner. Pardon my vagueness. Your effect on my mind is rather dramatic."

"Dinner. Oh." He traced her collarbones with the tip of his tongue before he answered.

Tess moaned. Her body felt deliciously heavy, and she sighed at the tingling sensation that scattered downward from his tongue. He slid his hand between her legs and stroked the moist folds there.

"Dinner was terrific," he declared. His mouth closed on the pulse point at the base of her throat, where he sucked gently for a moment. "And dessert was fantastic. I think I'll have seconds."

Soft New Age music, like starlight poured into sound, was playing on the cassette deck of Tess's stereo. The *Lady* shifted in the water from time to time, creaking slightly, soothingly. The wonderful man beside Tess raised his head and kissed her with a tenderness that made her sigh.

She tipped her head back and welcomed him. Life didn't get any better than this; confessions didn't get any easier.

"I'm not *falling* in love with you anymore," she whispered. "I'm in love with you. I love you."

He quivered against her. Rising on an elbow, he framed her face with his hand and looked down at her with somber, pain-filled eyes. Tess inhaled sharply.

"Oh, Jep, I said it too soon. . . ."

"I love you too."

She moaned with relief and happiness. Searching his eyes, Tess reveled in the adoration there but couldn't understand the sadness.

"What's wrong?" she asked, taking his face between her hands.

He shook his head in self-rebuke and smiled, easing his troubled look. "I've never said that before and meant it. It's a shocker."

She gasped softly. "Not in thirty-eight years?"

"Oh, I've meant it to my family—Kyle, Millie, my mother when I was about seven, not long before she died. I even told my Dad that I loved him, once. It embarrassed him. But no, I never put any commitment behind the words when I said them in the romantic sense. Until now. I don't ever want to lose you. That's a different kind of love from anything I've felt before."

"Well," she whispered, her throat burning from emotion, "I'll make sure that you don't regret saying it to me."

He sat up, pulled her into his arms, and held her with an intensity that brought a bittersweet ache to her chest. It was as if he'd found some kind of salvation.

At that moment Tess realized that she couldn't do anything to cheapen this great gift he'd given her.

Unless she trusted him with every secret she held dear, she didn't deserve him.

"I love you," she repeated, smiling against his shoulder. "And I have something very important that I want to share with you."

His arms tightened quickly, as if she'd startled him. He drew back and looked at her, his expression wary.

"Jep, relax," she said soothingly. "Wait here and I'll get it."

"Don't." His voice had an odd, strained quality. "Not right now."

Tess stroked his hair and smiled at him. "It won't take long. And then I'd like to make love with you again."

He let go of her reluctantly. She slipped into a cream-colored silk robe and went into the galley. There she opened the top door of the refrigerator, rearranged a stack of ice trays at the back of the freezer compartment, and removed the bottom one.

Standing at the kitchen's tiny sink she dumped an ice cube into her hand. Smiling in anticipation, she folded a kitchen towel and placed the ice cube on top of it. She left the galley with the towel cupped in both hands, like a sacred offering.

Jeopard sat on the edge of the bed, looking oddly tense, the coverlet wound around the lower half of his body.

"Jep, there's no need to be formal," she said teasingly, indicating the cover.

Tess sat down beside him and held her hands out proudly. Frozen in the center of the ice cube was a blue diamond the size of a marble.

"My secret," she said softly. "And now it's your secret too."

Jeopard stared at the melting cube. After a moment he almost laughed at the sick irony of it. The Iceman's hopes had been ruined by a damned ice cube.

Everything shut down inside him. It was a self-protective instinct, the same way he reacted whenever his life was in danger or a delicate situation had just become volatile.

Only this time, he never wanted to feel any emotion

again, because he knew the bitterness would eat him up.

"That's some trinket," he told her smoothly. "A present from Royce?"

"No. It belonged to my mother. My grandparents gave it to me on my eighteenth birthday."

The hell they did. It disappeared twenty years ago. Royce stole it. He left it to you.

Jeopard took the ice cube in his hand and squeezed it. Tiny rivulets of water ran down his wrist. Tess dabbed at them with the towel.

"Good heavens, Jep, do you have a fever?"

He opened his hand and looked down at the magnificent blue stone emerging from its prison of water. "Your mother must have been an incredibly successful pro skier if she could afford something like this."

Admit it, Tess. You know this came from the crown jewels of Kara. You know it's the Blue Princess.

"Oh, the diamond has been in the Kellgren family for three generations. Grandfather says it belonged to his mother."

Great story, Tess. Your sincere look is perfect.

"Honey, it must be worth a small fortune."

"Actually, it's not. Royce estimated the value at around thirty thousand dollars. A diamond as large as it ought to be worth a lot more. But it's got some flaws."

"Not to the average eye."

"No, but I can tell. I love it for the sentimental value more than anything else."

Jeopard felt as if some small wild animal were clawing to get out of his chest. "Why isn't it in a setting?"

"Grandfather said the old setting didn't do it justice, so he had it removed. I'll have a new one designed someday."

Yeah, kid, the setting would have made it easier to identify. "You aren't anxious to wear it?"

"I'd be too worried. It's valuable enough to make it worth stealing."

You ought to know, Tess. "Then why keep it on board the boat?"

She reached out and touched a fingertip to the glittering stone. "I never knew my mother. This makes me feel close to her."

And you can't risk putting it in a safe-deposit box. A nosy bank official might ask questions about such an unusual stone.

"Why are you showing it to me?" The last bit of ice melted under the diamond. It lay on Jeopard's palm, a pale blue teardrop that glittered even in the dim light. Disgusted by the feel of it, he dropped it onto the towel in Tess's hand.

She stared at him in confusion, looking a little hurt. "It's a whimsical secret of mine. I wanted to show you how much I trust you." She gave him a tentative smile. "My grandparents are worried that you're up to no good."

He forced himself to smile back as if that were the most unlikely thing he'd ever heard. "Tell them that your secret's safe with me."

Jeopard caught her chin, turned her to face him squarely, and asked in a teasing tone, "Any other secrets, Pocahontas?"

Royce. Tell me again that he was a retired diamond broker. Tell me again that he left everything to his daughters.

She searched his eyes so long that he knew she was worried about his strange mood. He could almost feel her withdrawing. "No," she said softly, and looked away.

Dammit, Tess. That hurt worse than anything.

He felt as if he were being torn inside out. He couldn't touch her, could barely look at her, and yet he knew he couldn't risk leaving. That would make her more wary.

"Honey?" he said in a low voice that aimed for gentleness.

She looked back at him, her eyes troubled. "Yes?"

"I'm a bastard for acting so unexcited. Thank you for sharing the diamond with me. It's just that I'm getting a killer headache. Remember that I mentioned I get migraines occasionally?"

"Oh, yes," she said happily, and exhaled with relief. "I mean, you had me worried there, Sundance. Poor man." She brushed her fingertips across his forehead. "Can I get you anything for it?"

"No. Maybe I can short-circuit it by going to sleep."

He grasped her hand and curled her fingers over the Blue Princess so that he wouldn't have to look at it anymore. "Go put that away. It concerns me that you keep something so valuable in an ice tray."

Her eyes filled with adoration. "You don't have to worry about me. I'm careful." She paused. "But I love you for worrying."

It was all Jeopard could do not to wince openly. What was she trying to do, destroy him? Had he met an equal at the game of deception he played so well?

"Get under the covers and relax," she murmured, stroking his neck. "Your muscles are full of knots! I'll give you a massage."

"No, I—"

"Come on, Jep. You can't tell me it won't help." She kissed him jauntily. "Into bed, Sundance. I'll be right back."

Miserable, he got into bed and lay on his stomach, his head burrowed in a pillow. She returned a few minutes later, turned off the desk lamp, and climbed into bed beside him. The white curtains let in a bit of light from the dock lamps, but still the darkness was blissfully deep.

Jeopard dug his fingers into the pillow as her warm, gentle hands slid over his shoulders. He replayed what he knew of her and realized that she had no reason to tell him that she loved him if it weren't the truth.

He ground his teeth. *Unless she knew what he was after and meant to sidetrack him.*

Jeopard considered that possibility for a long time, while she rubbed his neck and shoulders, occasionally bending forward to caress his back with a kiss. Each time she did, her breasts brushed against him.

"I feel a lot better," he said, lying. "Let's get some sleep."

She lay down close to him and rested one hand in the center of his back. "I love you, Jep," she whispered. "Good night."

"Good night." After a long hesitation, he swallowed hard and gave her the reply she wanted. "I love you too."

Damn, he was glad that she couldn't see his eyes. He hadn't cried in years.

She dreamed guilty dreams because she hadn't told Jeopard about Royce's being a jewel thief. She'd intended to tell the story after she showed him the blue diamond, but he'd looked at her so strangely that she'd faltered. And when she'd realized that he had a terrible headache, she'd decided to wait.

Tess woke up anxious to right her wrong. She reached for Jeopard and sat up sharply when she found him gone. Her heart pounding with a puzzling sense of dread, Tess squinted into a stream of early-morning sunshine that had slipped between a curtain and the air-conditioner.

He could be out jogging.

But he didn't jog—he hated it. He swam in the ocean every morning.

But he didn't swim this early.

He'd gone to the *Irresistible*, for some reason. He'd be right back.

Tess bounced out of bed, threw her robe around her shoulders, and went to the port window. Oh, how silly, this compulsion to open the curtains and look.

Okay, so she felt silly that morning. Tess raked the curtains back.

The *Irresistible* was gone.

A stunned minute later she gasped out loud and ran to the kitchen.

Her blue diamond was gone too.

Jeopard arrived in Los Angeles by 8:00 A.M., less than an hour after he handed the yacht's key to a man who worked for Olaf.

He thought that his driving time from Long Beach was particularly good, considering his unplanned stop beside the freeway, where he'd hunched over a guard rail and regretted the four cups of strong coffee he'd poured into his stomach.

Coffee and misery didn't mix well.

He was met in the lobby of a sleek L.A. hotel by a lanky, well-dressed wolfhound of a man with enormous gray eyes and long blond hair. The man had already registered Jeopard under a false name.

The wolfhound shooed the bellmen away and carried one of Jeopard's suitcases himself. Jeopard carried the other two. He and the wolfhound didn't speak at all as they rode a glass-paneled elevator and walked to the hotel room.

Once inside, Jeopard pulled the blue diamond from the pocket of his sports coat. He tossed it to the man, who exhaled visibly with relief. Jeopard received a check for ten thousand dollars in return. It was the second half of his and Kyle's fee.

"I wish you'd taken another day," the man said wistfully. "I've grown to like Los Angeles while I've been waiting for you. Tomorrow I was going to Burbank to see the Johnny Carson show."

"Sorry."

"She won't contact the police?" the wolfhound asked in a heavy Swedish accent. Swedish was Kara's official language.

Jeopard had always suspected that Olaf's top aide was an idiot. That question confirmed it. "She isn't going to report that someone stole her stolen diamond."

"Ah. Yes."

"And you won't attempt to prosecute her."

"Correct. We have nothing to gain. Plus it would be difficult to prove that she knew the diamond was stolen."

"All right. Then we're done."

The wolfhound smiled slyly. "Tell me, did she live up to her reputation? I have many photographs besides those I gave you in the report. So many pictures of her in swimsuits. What remarkable legs! A man could easily imagine them wrapped around him. . . . Pardon me. I've offended you."

Jeopard never said a word. He simply looked up at the man until all the color drained from the face beneath the fine, flowing hair. The wolfhound bowed slightly and backed toward the door as if he were afraid to turn his back.

"Your work is excellent, Mr. Surprise," he said in a

small, strained voice. "And I'm glad we'll have no more need of you."

He slipped out the door and slammed it behind him. Jeopard didn't move until he heard the last faint footfall as the man hurried away.

Then he slumped on the side of the bed and put his head in his hands.

It was just as well that she'd loaned the Jaguar to Brandt for the week. Driving would have been dangerous in her current emotional state. Running wasn't much safer.

Tess covered the three miles to her grandparents' duplex in record time. When she fell against the low wall of their terrace, gasping desperately for breath, her heels were blistered and her insteps ached from running in ordinary tennis shoes without benefit of socks.

Her faded UCLA T-shirt was soaked with sweat, and her cut-off jeans bore bloodstains where she'd wiped her scraped palms after she tripped on a curb.

Before she could stagger up the tiled steps to the front door, her grandparents saw her from the living-room window. Their faces contorted with anxiety, Viktoria and Karl met Tess halfway up the steps and practically carried her inside.

She slumped on their couch and stared numbly at the floor while Viktoria hovered over her, dabbing her face with a cool washcloth. Karl sat down and took her hand.

"What is it, *raring*?" he implored.

"He stole the blue diamond," she answered wretchedly. "Jeopard Surprise."

Their audible gasps made her wince with humiliation and sorrow. Tess knew that her pain would worsen as soon as she fully comprehended the words she'd just spoken. Just then nothing seemed real.

"I showed it to him last night. He . . . he took it while I was asleep. His yacht was gone this morning."

Tess looked from Karl to Viktoria, watching their faces as they absorbed her news. Their expressions seemed frantic. "I love . . . loved him," she said in a choked voice. "And I thought he loved me."

"But you knew him only days!" Viktoria exclaimed, wringing her hands.

"Yes." Tess hung her head. She couldn't explain why there'd seemed nothing foolish about loving a man she'd known for such a short time.

"We were having him checked out," Karl muttered. "But now, it's too late."

Tess froze. "Checked out?"

"I have friends at the American embassy in Stockholm. I asked for their help. They know people who can find out anything about American citizens. We haven't heard from them yet."

Tess clenched her fists. "What's going on? Why did you suspect Jeopard from the start?"

Viktoria sank into a chair and covered her face. "Oh, Karl, Karl. We are lost."

Tess rubbed her forehead. Shards of pain shot through her scalp. Nothing made sense. She almost strangled on the next words. "I have to call the police."

Viktoria burst into tears. "No. Oh, Karl. Tell her."

Tess stared at her grandmother in confusion. "What?"

"You can't go to the police," Karl murmured wearily.

Tess straightened, her pulse roaring in her ears. "Why not?"

"The diamond is . . . not safe."

Tess pinched the bridge of her nose and fought the urge to scream. "Why, grandfather?" she asked patiently.

Viktoria and Karl traded a long, covert look. "Because we stole it from someone twenty years ago," Karl said slowly, his eyes never leaving his wife's. "And now perhaps that someone wants it back."

Jeopard lay on the hotel bed, his hands behind his head. Beyond the room's picture window Los Angeles sweated under a smoggy sky. The late-afternoon sun sifted through the smog and made the room hot.

Jeopard hadn't changed clothes, hadn't unpacked, hadn't even bothered to take off his sports coat. He was sweating, but not from the heat.

This time the Iceman had lost. He couldn't just walk away; he could only admit defeat and surrender.

The following day he'd go back to Long Beach, tell Tess everything, beg, coax, and seduce her into telling him everything in return, then try his best to win her trust again. If she could accept his work he could accept her past.

And they'd both start new, together.

Seven

"Yo, Tess. Want a doughnut while you stare at the sunrise?"

Tess roused herself from the chair on the *Lady*'s aft deck. She hadn't slept at all, her body felt caved in, and she was certain her shapeless T-shirt and wrinkled shorts qualified her for a slob award.

Brandt stood on the dock, grinning and holding up a box from one of the local doughnut franchises. "I brought the Jag back last night, but you weren't around," he called. "I've got something to show you. You're gonna love it."

Moving like an old woman, Tess met him on the dock. She gazed at Brandt distractedly. Her throat felt rusty, and she was glad he couldn't see her eyes behind the dark sunglasses she wore.

The love of her life was a con artist, and her grandparents were jewel thieves. Sure, she felt like being entertained at that moment.

"Another electronic toy?" she croaked, glancing at the device Brandt held in the hand not occupied by a doughnut box.

"Yeah. Just finished it this week. It's bitchin', Tess. Politicians in Third World countries use this kind of stuff to protect themselves from terrorists. Watch."

He pointed toward the marina parking lot. Through a haze of disinterest Tess noted that he'd parked the Jaguar in a good spot next to the curb. Brandt was an ultraresponsible teenager, and she didn't worry about loaning him her pride and joy.

Brandt held up his new plaything, which resembled a walkie-talkie. "Press a button, and . . . all right!"

The Jaguar's engine purred to life, and the headlights flashed on. "Ignition by remote control!" he announced happily.

And then the Jaguar exploded.

Jeopard caught the midmorning news update as he was dressing to leave the hotel. He halted in front of the TV and stared at the screen with cold horror. He saw the Sun Cove Marina sign in the background. In the foreground was a television reporter beside the burned, twisted ruins of a car.

". . . again, Los Angeles city attorney Suzanne Burdett, vacationing in Long Beach, was slightly injured by flying metal when a car exploded in a parking lot where she was jogging early this morning.

"She was treated and released from a Long Beach hospital. Luckily the car's owner, Tess Gallatin, wasn't in the car at the time. She told me that she was testing a remote-control ignition device designed by a friend when the car exploded. Experts from the Long Beach Police bomb squad said evidence indicates that the bombing was the work of a professional.

"There are no leads in the case. More details at noon. For Eyewitness News, this is Rena Brown, Long Beach."

Five seconds later Jeopard was on the phone, calling Tess's number at her grandparents' house. Her dulcet voice came to him via the recording on her answering machine.

"This is Jeopard," he said calmly. "Check into a hotel under my name and lock yourself in a room. Don't come out. I'm in L.A. It's ten A.M. I'm leaving for Long Beach right now. I'll find you."

He prayed that she'd check the answering machine sometime soon. Next he called Kyle. In Florida it was 7:00 A.M. Kyle was barely awake.

"What? Jep?"

"Olaf's people may be trying to kill Tess Gallatin."

That cleared Kyle's fog. The mellow jokester snapped to alert. "You got a tip?"

"Somebody wired her car this morning."

"Was she hurt?"

"No. God help Olaf if she were."

Kyle's stunned silence greeted that remark. Finally he asked, "Personal?"

"Yes."

"She's hiding something else," Kyle said musingly. "They want her quiet."

"Yeah. I know less about her past than I thought. Doesn't matter. If they want her, they'll have to kill me first."

"What?"

"I love her. I'm going back to Long Beach and get her out of there."

"*You love her?*"

"If anything happens to me, make certain she's protected, Kyle."

"You love—all right."

"Call Drake. I'll need him."

Kyle whistled softly. "You *are* serious."

Jeopard slammed the phone down, then grabbed his wallet, the keys to his rental car, and the loaded Magnum .44.

Jeopard was trying to kill her.

Tess sat in her grandparents' living room, hugging herself. Karl paced. Viktoria sat by the telephone, staring at the answering machine as if Jeopard's voice were the essence of evil.

"It's a trick," Karl said grimly. "The man must think we're fools."

Tess shuddered. She wanted to curl up and hibernate until the world made sense again. It might take years.

"He doesn't know that we learned about his background," she said wearily. They knew all about Jeopard Surprise now. Karl had gotten in touch with his sources and demanded whatever information they had.

A dull sense of horror was the only emotion that kept

Tess from feeling empty. She'd fallen in love with a cold-blooded assassin.

Jeopard Surprise was a mercenary in the worst sense of the word. He'd made a career out of killing people for pay. His wholesome businessman's image was a complete lie.

Someone wanted the blue diamond and then wanted her dead, and had sent an expert to take care of the job. An expert who knew how to capture her heart and soul to make his task easier. Now Tess realized that the coldness in his eyes had hidden indescribable cruelty.

"I don't understand," she said raggedly. "Why does he have to kill me? He's got the diamond. What did I do?"

"No more time for talk," Karl interjected. "We'll get out of the country. Mama, go pack. We'll go home. In Stockholm I'll find help to fight this monster."

"No! It's all our fault," Viktoria cried. "We'll call the police and tell them everything. Then they can protect Tess."

Tess rose proudly and looked at her grandparents. "No. You wanted to give me something no one else had—a queen's diamond. I've been struggling to understand how grief over my mother's death provoked you to steal the diamond from the Queen of Kara. I'm trying to understand your need for revenge after Mother was killed on a poorly designed ski slope in Kara."

Tess paused, thinking. "I was married to a retired jewel thief, and I loved him. I love you guys, too, and I won't let you martyr yourselves. I guess it's just my destiny to love people who steal diamonds."

Oh, Jeopard.

Tess took a deep breath. "I'm half Cherokee Indian. My father's people are survivors. Warriors. I'm not leaving without my medallion and my amulet. I'll go back to the boat and get them right now."

"No!" Karl cried. Viktoria clasped her heart.

"I have time before Jeopard gets here. I'll take your car—we know it's safe. This is something I have to do for my great-great-grandmother. Katherine Gallatin wouldn't be intimidated by *anything*, and neither will I."

Karl and Viktoria looked absolutely stricken. Tess grabbed the keys to their station wagon and left before she could think too much about her fear.

If the guy was a salesman, then Jeopard was Mr. Rogers.

As Jeopard got out of the rental car his attention remained riveted to the neatly dressed man who strolled along the marina's dock carrying a thick satchel with *Ask Me About Happy Suds Cleaning Products*! stenciled on the side.

Jeopard's nerves tingled. Moving gracefully, he walked down a flight of stairs that led from the parking lot to the dock.

The Happy Suds salesman paused by various boats, casually studied a note in his hand, and moved on. When a voluptuous woman wearing a T-shirt over a bikini waved at him, he waved back but kept walking.

The guy was no salesman, Jeopard knew without doubt.

Every muscle poised for action, Jeopard ambled down the dock behind the visitor. A hard, deadly tightness came over him as the man stopped in front of the *Lady*.

Jeopard glanced back. Madam Voluptuous had gone into her boat's cabin. No one else was around on this weekday morning.

The man lifted his satchel and fiddled with something on the handle. Then he crossed the gangplank and stepped onto the *Lady*'s bow.

Tess's security alarm didn't make a sound.

Jeopard realized immediately that the visitor's satchel held something besides samples. He had just counteracted the *Lady*'s alarm system. A thorough professional.

"Hey, pal," Jeopard yelled. He staggered down the dock, weaving dangerously close to the wooden buffers at the edge. "You got a light?"

The man, a short, stocky redhead with a wholesome face straight out of a Norman Rockwell painting, turned and frowned at Jeopard. "You're drunk."

"Hell, you're kiddin'. I thought we were having another earthquake."

"Beat it. I'm busy."

Jeopard reached the *Lady*'s gangplank and staggered aboard, flapping at his coat pockets. "Damn. No cigarettes. Come on, buddy. If you got 'em, share one."

"I'm afraid I don't—"

"Too bad," Jeopard interjected, and rabbit-punched him in the jaw.

The skilled upper cut made the ersatz salesman collapse like a bad soufflé, and he tumbled onto the deck. His coat fell open to reveal a small handgun with a silencer.

Jeopard knelt beside the man, jerked the gun from its holster, and tossed it over the *Lady*'s railing. "Son of a bitch," he whispered to the unconscious man. Jeopard propped the satchel on his chest. "You're lucky I don't have time to deal with you."

He didn't have *any* time. Jeopard heard a quick creaking sound and looked down the stairwell just as the cabin door banged open. Tess stood there, staring up at him, an expression of fear and horror on her face.

Jeopard could imagine how confused she must be, seeing him crouched over an unconscious salesman who had a small billboard on his chest innocently advising the world to ask him about Happy Suds Cleaning Products.

"Don't be misled," Jeopard told her in a soothing voice. "I'm the guy in the white hat. Relax, honey."

She raised a tiny pistol and pointed it at his chest.

"The Cherokees had a title for a female who was good at fighting," she informed him imperiously. " 'War Woman.' "

Jeopard straightened slowly and held up both hands. "Tess. I know you have a lot of doubts, but I'm your only hope."

"You're a hired killer."

Faltering at that abrupt charge, Jeopard stared at her in stunned silence.

"I know about you," she continued, the lethal little gun trembling in her hands. "You were hired to steal the diamond and get rid of me."

The accusation that he was a paid assassin—paid to

kill the brightest hope that had ever come into his life—made him continue to look at her in astonishment.

"Who told you that?"

"My grandfather had you checked out. He has friends in America diplomatic circles."

Jeopard grimaced inwardly. There were no official government records on former high-level agents such as himself. There were only carefully constructed facades designed to alarm and deceive an enemy.

The truth about his former line of work was disturbing enough; the lies she'd been given must have terrified her. But maybe he needed that advantage right now.

"Tess, we haven't got much time. We have to get out of here."

"So you can take care of me without anyone's seeing you?" Her voice cracked. "Who hired you?"

The assassin stirred weakly under Jeopard's feet. Time had run out. Now that this guy had been exposed, someone else would be after her.

Jeopard watched Tess glance downward at the fallen man. He used that unguarded moment to lunge for her. She yelped, lowered the gun, and tried to shove her cabin door shut. Jeopard plowed through and wrapped both arms around her.

The momentum carried them both to her bed, where he fell on top of her. The gun sailed out of her hand and struck her computer with a metallic thud.

Jeopard pinned her arms and legs down. "The gun wasn't loaded," he told her gruffly. "I could see the empty chambers."

Her silver-blue eyes were as fierce as they were frightened. "You cruel, deceiving bastard. Where were you when you called my answering machine? It would have taken you an hour to get here from Los Angeles."

"I came by helicopter."

She inhaled harshly. "My grandparents will look for me."

"By the time they start, you'll be gone. And later you'll call and tell them that you were wrong about me, that you've gone into hiding with me until the danger blows over."

She wiggled under him. "No."

"Yes. I have a recording of your voice. That night we talked at the Zanzi Bar I recorded you for *hours*. My people can copy your speech patterns and tones from that. Someone will call Karl and Viktoria for you. Your grandparents will hear you say that everything's just fine between you and me."

She groaned and gritted her teeth. "What do you want from me?"

"I'm trying to save your life."

"Tell me the truth!"

"Neither of us is interested in the truth. You've made that clear. You're hiding something that makes somebody want to kill you. If you'd told me everything about the diamond, you wouldn't be in this predicament."

"I told you!"

She writhed under him like a trapped cat. Jeopard knew a dozen different techniques that would subdue her, but none that wouldn't hurt like hell.

He squeezed his legs around hers and clasped her wrists in an iron grip above her head. "Stop it. Stop it, Tess, or by God I'll make you sorry."

She froze, then began quivering at the lethal insinuation in his tone. Jeopard gazed down at her coldly, all reconciliation gone from his manner. He watched her eyes widen in alarm at the look on his face. His heart broke.

He'd pay a price for saving her. He could see it in her disgust and terror.

Jeopard rolled her onto her stomach, so he wouldn't have to look at her eyes. He used his belt to bind her hands behind her back, then went to her small dresser and searched until he found two long silk scarves.

He tied her ankles together with one of them, then knotted the other one snugly around her neck. Jeopard turned her over, winced inside at the wretched look on her face, and lifted her toward the head of the bed.

He fastened the end of the neck binding to the bedstead.

"Tied like a dog to a post," she whispered raggedly. "At least give me a fighting chance."

"Be quiet."

He left the cabin before he lost all sense of logic, ripped the bindings off of her, and begged her to understand what he was trying to do.

The hired killer sat up groggily. Jeopard knelt in front of him, grasped him by the collar, and smiled at him.

"If you'd hurt her, I'd have made you regret it," he told the man in a soft, pleasant voice. "If I had time and privacy, I'd make you regret even *thinking* about hurting her. But you're in luck. As it is, I'll simply describe you in detail to some very ruthless people who like to take justice into their own hands. Now, get up, walk off this boat, and don't look back. I'll be watching."

The man took his satchel and left without a word. Jeopard tracked him with a shrewd gaze, memorizing everything about him, until he got into a small sedan and drove away.

Back in the cabin Tess had turned to lie on her side, and her neck was bent at an awkward angle because of the way she was tied to the bed. "Don't touch me," she said in a low, raspy tone as he slid a pillow under her head.

Her chest moved swiftly. Jeopard groaned with frustration—she was about to attempt screams that a Banshee might envy. He ran to get more scarves, then stuffed one into her mouth and used another to tie it in place. She made muffled protests and tried to twist her head away from him.

Dull despair washed over Jeopard. She'd never believe his reasons for doing this. He grasped her jaw and forced her to look up at him.

"I'm taking the boat out to sea. Someone will meet us there. You might as well stop fighting, because you're trapped."

She jerked her head away and shut her eyes, effectively dismissing him. Jeopard touched a fingertip to the medallion that lay on her right breast, then lifted the antler amulet and looked at it.

A lump rose in his throat. What had she been trying to do, ward him off as though he were an evil spirit?

She still had her eyes shut, finding him too loathsome to look at.

Perhaps he was evil, and it was too late to save himself. But he'd save her, even if it meant putting her through hell to do it.

Jeopard grimly tossed the amulet back on her chest. "You won't need any Cherokee magic," he told her curtly. "As long as you do what I tell you, you won't get hurt."

Feeling sick, he left her to ponder that heartless warning and went above to set sail.

The next two hours were an endless horror. Wherever Jeopard was taking her, it would be far away from anyone who could help her.

First they were met by a small power boat piloted by a middle-aged man who shook Jeopard's hand but never said a word. They were transferred to the boat, and Tess looked back forlornly at the *Swedish Lady*, sitting abandoned.

"The Coast Guard will find her," Jeopard said brusquely, and pulled her around so that she couldn't look anymore.

The power boat took them up the coast to an unused oil platform, where a helicopter waited. There was another man, who shook Jeopard's hand as if they'd done this sort of thing many times—which they must have, Tess thought bitterly.

The helicopter took them inland to a stretch of empty desert, where a small private plane sat alone on a windswept highway. The pilot smiled at her as Jeopard carried her—still bound hand and foot—onto the plane.

Since Jeopard had long since removed the stuffing from her mouth, she told the pilot that he'd go to prison for aiding a kidnapper. He smiled even more broadly.

Jeopard spoke to her with a minimum of cool, brusque words. He put her in a window seat and sat beside her, his side pressed tightly to hers. After the plane settled into its cruising altitude he untied her.

"Rest room is in the back. Now's your chance."

"How kind of you."

She rose and swept past him without a backward glance. When she returned he motioned her back to the window seat.

"Sit down. All right. Hands on your lap."

Then he carefully prepared to bind her wrists and ankles with strips of wide, soft tape. She'd be more comfortable but no less a prisoner.

Tess stared out the window at clouds and blue sky, her teeth clenched. He handled her with a businesslike intimacy that made her face burn with fury and humiliation. Damn the man!

He rubbed her wrists to make certain they weren't chafed, then probed gently at her scraped palms. He ran his hand down her ankle and lifted one sandaled foot to study the big blister on her heel. Then he sat back and scrutinized the wrinkled shorts and old T-shirt she'd worn for the past twenty-four hours. Finally he put two fingers at the base of her throat and checked her pulse.

"Now I know how a slave girl feels in a harem," she said between gritted teeth. "Do you intend to molest me later?"

He withdrew his hand slowly. "Of course. I'm that kind of man, as you well know. It wouldn't look good for my reputation if I didn't do a little sordid molesting, now would it?"

She flinched but said nothing.

"Your face is gaunt. I want you to eat," he announced.

"A fattened pig for the sacrifice."

He went to an ice chest in the front of the cabin and brought her a carton of milk, a large piece of cheese, two apples, and a package of crackers, all of which he placed on her lap.

He opened the milk carton and wedged it between her hands.

"Eat. If you need help, say so."

"Let's get something straight. You disgust me. I won't ask you for anything."

"You will soon enough," he said softly, and left her shivering as he went forward to sit with the pilot.

• • •

Two hours later the plane landed on an airstrip set in a valley among dry, barren mountains Tess couldn't identify. She blanched as Jeopard carried her out of the plane and she saw a small private jet on the runway.

"How far are we going?"

His arms tightened around her. "I got a terrific idea from your Cherokee history lessons. We're going to North Carolina. Remember the caves in the mountains there? We're going to hide in one."

"Hide from what?" she asked in a small, stunned voice.

"That's for you to tell me. You know why somebody's trying to kill you. I don't."

Tess shook her head fiercely. "You're the only killer."

"Enough." Jeopard stopped in the middle of the runway. He looked down at her, his blue eyes icy. "When you're ready to tell me the truth, talk to me. Otherwise, keep quiet."

Tess swallowed hard. She didn't understand his frightening game. After he carried her aboard the jet and deposited her in a seat, she looked up at him desperately.

"Do you want money? A ransom? Is this revenge for the diamond?" She gasped. "You wouldn't hurt my grandparents! Please tell me you don't intend to do anything to them!"

He stared down at her with tired, unhappy eyes. "I'm not interested in them. Only in you. And you can make this a helluva lot easier if you'll open up. Tell me how you got the Blue Princess."

"The what?" she asked plaintively. "You mean the blue diamond? I told you, they gave it to me for my eighteenth birthday! I'd never seen it before then! But I forgive them for what they did! They had reasons—"

"Dammit, stop," he said, bending over her with menace. His expression was deadly. "I know that Royce was a jewel thief. The sooner you talk, the sooner this will be over with."

Tess's head reeled. He had known about Royce all along. *The sooner you talk, the sooner this will be over with.* When he got his information, would he dispose of her? But what information? And what did Royce have to do with the blue diamond that Jeopard called the Blue Princess?

Silence was obviously her best defense.

Tess met his gaze stoically. He scrutinized her for nearly a minute, as if he were trying to force a reaction from her. She barely blinked.

Finally, fatigue and dismay clouded his expression. He chuckled, then told her in a low, tense tone, "All right, Pocahontas, if you want war, you've got it."

They lost three hours of daylight flying east, and when they landed, darkness had fallen. Tess couldn't see much beyond the jet's windows, but she glimpsed tall outlines and suspected that they must be in the North Carolina mountains.

Jeopard and the pilot disappeared outside for a long time. Tess caught glimmers from their flashlights and peered into the night. She thought she saw a third man. Yes.

When Jeopard came back on board he was followed by a muscular black-haired giant with a handsome face that might have been carved from a granite block. Tess gaped. The man had to stoop to negotiate the cabin ceiling. He was easily seven feet tall. He wore western boots, faded jeans, and a khaki safari shirt.

A huge knife was strapped to his belt.

Jeopard, his face unreadable, gestured casually from Tess to the giant. "Drake Lancaster."

She and the giant shared a speculative look. "Nice to meet you," he said politely in a rumbling bass voice. It was as if the mountains themselves had spoken to her.

Tess arched a brow at him and said nothing.

"She's taken a vow of silence," Jeopard noted drolly. "It's nothing personal. As far as I know she still listens, even if she won't answer."

Jeopard leaned against a seat and crossed his arms over his chest. Lancaster sat down in the aisle and rested his hands on his updrawn knees. "Ms. Gallatin, I brought you some clothes and other necessities. In the morning I'll take you and Jeopard into the mountains on horseback. You need to get a good night's sleep. And please relax. You're safe."

When she didn't answer, he shifted awkwardly and looked at Jeopard for help.

"I think she likes you," Jeopard quipped. "She didn't hiss."

The huge man sighed as if he didn't understand these kind of man/woman games very well. He reached into a shirt pocket and retrieved something. "Before I forget. Take a look at this, man. What a gorgeous doll. Rucker and Dinah sent this to me last week."

Tess craned her head as Jeopard reached for what appeared to be a photograph. Gorgeous doll? Some femme fatale, probably.

Jeopard gazed at the photo, and a gentle smile touched his mouth. She watched him with dull intrigue, wondering what woman could draw such tenderness from him.

Sincere tenderness, not the fake kind he'd shown her.

Jeopard glanced over at her. "My goddaughter," he told her, and held out a photograph of a smiling baby in a pink pinafore.

"Mine too," Drake interjected firmly.

Tess studied the photograph, then let her eyes flicker up slowly to Jeopard's with what she hoped was a distinctly uninterested expression.

"You've heard of Rucker McClure, the writer?" he asked.

She nodded.

"Drake and I helped him rescue his wife and daughter last year. The details are classified, but suffice it to say, we were quite proud of ourselves."

Tess lifted her chin and eyed Jeopard coolly. She couldn't resist taunting his inflated ego. "Am I supposed to be impressed because you two professional killers have a soft spot for children? Sorry, I'm not."

She caught Drake Lancaster's look of astonishment. He turned toward Jeopard. "What does she think—"

"She got my official background."

"Oh." Drake frowned.

"It's a little difficult to prove otherwise at this point."

"Right."

"So she thinks I'm worse than I am. And you're guilty by association."

"My mother warned me not to hang around with people like you."

"Yes. Undoubtedly."

Jeopard straightened. Tess found his gaze back on her. It was challenging but somehow extremely sad. She felt bewildered and exhausted. What new con was he trying to pull?

"Time for bed, Pocahontas." He gestured toward the tape around her wrists and feet. "Drake, get rid of this."

Drake got up, crouched over her, and sliced the tape with careful strokes of his huge knife. Then he left the plane, his head bent awkwardly to avoid denting the roof.

Jeopard grasped her wrist. "Let's go. There's a sleeping bag waiting outside for you."

"Are we sharing, godfather?" she asked tautly.

"No. I wouldn't want to fall asleep while my throat was within reach of your hands."

He led her out of the jet. Tess looked around, smelled the rich, cool night air of the mountains, then glanced down at the concrete under her feet. "Drug trafficking," she said harshly. "That's the only reason you'd have these hidden runways."

"I don't sell, buy, or use drugs. You've watched too many episodes of *Miami Vice*."

He drew her across an open field toward a campfire at the edge of the forest. The pilot lay on a sleeping bag, swigging a soft drink. Drake Lancaster knelt beside the fire, stirring something in a pot set among the embers.

Several horses were tethered to nearby trees. Tess gazed around at the blackness outside the ring of firelight. In the glow of a half-moon the craggy, forested peaks seemed as mysterious to her as the masterful blond man who had hold of her wrist.

"Welcome to the Nantahala Mountains," Jeopard told her.

He guided her to a sleeping bag at the edge of the firelight. It lay near the base of a large dogwood tree.

"Sit down." He looked over his shoulder. "Drake, did you remember the chain?"

Her heart pounding with dread, Tess lowered herself and sat cross-legged. Chain? Drake Lancaster went to a canvas bag and pulled out a long, slender silver chain. He brought it to Jeopard, along with two small padlocks.

"Here's the key," he said, and dropped it into the side pocket of Jeopard's sports coat.

Tess stared at the chain in horror. She shivered inwardly as Jeopard looped it around her neck and fastened the impromptu collar with a padlock. He took the other end to the dogwood tree and locked it around the trunk.

Then he merely glanced at her and walked away to join his friends.

She numbly pushed the chain out of her way, turned to face the mountains, and hugged her knees to her chest. Only the most rigid pride kept her from crying. Tess dug her fingers into her bare legs and stared into the forest.

The medallion and the antler amulet pressed into her breasts, and the feel of them made a bittersweet chill run down her spine.

This was Cherokee land, the Sun Land of the tribe's mythology, and she had ancestral spirits on her side that Jeopard Surprise couldn't begin to battle. She belonged there, and he didn't. She didn't care what he did to her. She was strong.

Tess caught the low murmur of Drake's voice and heard Jeopard's laughter. Despair engulfed her.

Who was she kidding? She was miserable.

There was only one reason why she felt so hurt and betrayed by Jeopard's treatment. She didn't want to love him anymore, and her agony came from knowing that she still did.

Eight

The chain was a hard, rattling weight hanging between her shoulder blades. Tess looped it over one elbow so that it wouldn't tug so much on the tender flesh of her neck. She slid a hand under the steel links and gingerly rubbed her chafed, sweating skin.

Tess shifted in her saddle and thought about the other chafed parts of her body. She glanced over her shoulder and glimpsed Jeopard, whose horse stayed close behind hers. She sensed that he was watching her, as usual. His unwavering attention seemed designed to force her to notice him in return.

Tess faced forward proudly and pretended to study their surroundings. The air was sweet and the scenery spectacular, which made her situation seem even more depressing. Startled insects hummed louder as the horses' feet crunched through the undergrowth.

To her right the land dropped into a beautiful, dramatic gorge. Massive granite boulders overhung the banks of a stream bed at the bottom, and thick, graceful trees draped their limbs toward the rushing water.

Nantahala meant "land of the noonday sun" in Cherokee, because the mountains rose so steeply that some of the narrow passes between them stayed in shadow most of the day. The name also belonged to a river in the area that was popular with white-water aficionados.

Drake, trying awkwardly to chat with her that morning, had mentioned that they were on the edge of the

Great Smoky Mountains National Forest and that the Nantahala River was no more than five miles from the landing strip. White-water enthusiasts flocked to the area to raft, canoe, and kayak during the summer. There was a small town in the vicinity.

Tess chewed on her lower lip and considered that information. Civilization was within walking distance. A long walk, but she could make it. Of course, for the past two hours Drake had led them farther from civilization and deeper into the national forest along winding, nearly indistinct trails.

Let's see, she thought. She could follow the sun back. No, she could barely see the sun. Wasn't there some rule about moss growing on the north side of a tree? Or was it the south side?

Landmarks. Tess looked around. Yes, there were thousands of them. Trees. Identical trees. She sighed with dismay. Weren't Indians instinctively supposed to know their way through the woods?

She ran her fingers under the chain again and winced at the raw prickling sensation on her throat.

"Here. Take this."

Jeopard nudged his horse up beside hers on the narrow mountain trail. He pulled a soft red bandanna from the back pocket of his jeans and handed it to her. "Wrap that around your neck."

Tess eyed him coolly. Drake had supplied them both with basic clothing for this venture: jeans, leather hiking shoes, and loose cotton shirts with short sleeves. But he hadn't known her size, and apparently liked to think everyone was as large as himself.

If the wind caught her just right, her jeans would inflate and *float* her to safety. At least her shoes and socks fit.

Jeopard, on the other hand, looked like the Esquire Man at a cattle roundup. His tousled blond hair gave him a deceptively boyish charm, his light blue shirt bore no sweat stains, and his jeans maintained a neat crease down the center of each lean, muscular leg. Head 'em up and move 'em out, Calvin Klein, Tess thought sarcastically.

Tess ignored the bandanna as she'd ignored every

gesture, word, and look of his all morning. She gazed disdainfully at the chain looped around his saddle horn. He kept her on a leash, but the last thing she'd be was his pet.

"Either tie this bandanna around your neck or I'll tie it for you," he ordered calmly.

"If you're going to kill me, why do you care about my comfort?"

"Drake! Hold up a minute!"

Drake reined his horses in and looked curiously over his shoulder. Jeopard reached out, grabbed the chain between her shoulder blades, and pulled her toward him with even, firm force.

Her horse felt the off-center shift of her body and halted, sidestepping until it bumped Jeopard's horse to a stop too. Tess clung to the saddle horn and tried not to fall off. When her face was only inches from Jeopard's and her leg was mashed securely against his from knee to hip, he tucked the bandanna around her neck. His warning blue eyes held her defensive ones.

"I've killed people," he told her in a low, controlled tone. "But I'm not a *killer*. I've done some ugly things, but I've done them for good reasons. That doesn't make me a saint, but I'm not a monster, either. I'm not going to hurt you."

His tense, heartfelt words made goose bumps scatter down Tess's arms. She searched his face desperately, not knowing what to believe. She couldn't ignore him any longer. "Then who blew up my car?"

"Possibly the people who hired me. I don't know." His jaw tightened. "How many people have reason to want revenge against you and Royce?"

She stared at him open-mouth. "Me and Royce? I wasn't involved in Royce's profession. He was retired."

"And Royce didn't leave you anything in his will?"

"I told you that he didn't!"

"Except for the Blue Princess."

Tess bit each word off emphatically. "I told you, my grandparents *gave* me the diamond on my eighteenth birthday. They stole it from Queen Isabella of Kara because of some misguided urge for revenge. My mother died in an accident on a ski slope at a Karan resort."

"That's a ridiculous story. I had your grandparents checked out after they came to the marina and spied on me. They wouldn't steal an apple from the corner grocery."

Tess shivered with frustration. On that point she agreed with him. The story still perplexed her.

"I thought *you* weren't capable of stealing from *me*. I thought you were a Florida businessman on vacation. I thought *you* were someone very special."

"I retrieved your *stolen* diamond for its owner. Don't play games with me. You knew the diamond was hot, and that Royce was the one who stole it."

She shook both fists at him. "I'm telling you the truth, which is more than you ever told me! You were paid to get close to me, and you weren't particular about the way you did it!"

He inhaled sharply. "I love you. Even if you're still determined to lie about your past."

"Oh, stop!" she demanded in disgust and shock. Tess pulled back from him, her eyes full of tears. She held the chain out defiantly. "Is this how you treat someone you love?"

"When it's the only way to make her do what's best for her, yes."

"I don't need that kind of love."

"You need to stay alive, don't you? And I intend to keep you that way while my brother and Drake try to learn who the hell wants you dead. It would be helpful if you'd give me some clues."

Her shoulders slumped. "I've told you all I know."

"Dammit, I might as well talk to the mountains." He waved curtly to Drake, who started up the trail again.

Tess slanted a look at him. "You'd better learn how, if you want friendly conversation."

Jeopard urged his horse ahead of hers and tugged on her chain. "Move it. The sooner you tell me the truth and make friends, the sooner I can let you off this leash."

Tess bit back bitter words that would only antagonize him more and hurried her horse after his. The chain stretched between them like a bond neither could escape.

• • •

For a cave, it was cozy.

It looked as though some giant had scooped a handful of rock from the mountain's side. There was nothing dank or dark about the cave; it had a wide, tall entrance that let in a lot of the afternoon sun. The floor was fairly level and the walls had a whitish limestone surface.

Tess stood at the entrance and gazed outward at a vista of gently rounded blue-green mountains. The ground sloped for a hundred feet in front of the cave, then dropped gradually toward a distant valley.

"It's like looking out a window at the top of the world," Drake observed as he began unloading gear from the pack horse.

"Get used to the view," Jeopard told her. He took his end of her chain to a stout young maple tree growing by the cave's entrance. There he knelt and padlocked the chain into place.

The chain was easily thirty feet long, so Tess could walk to the center of the cave or well outside the entrance. But it was a short tether, considering her humiliation and anger.

She sat down on a rocky outcropping and stared into the distance, her back aching with the attempt to maintain her dignity, her thoughts turbulent. Jeopard refused to believe her story about the blue diamond, he claimed to be on her side, and yet he intended to keep her chained in a cave, at his beck and call.

And he'd said that he loved her.

"Here. Make yourself useful. Blow up these air mattresses."

Jeopard dropped a heap of plastic and a bicycle pump onto the ground in front of her, then walked away. Her mouth clamped tightly shut, Tess went to work.

While she was inflating the first mattress, angrily stamping the foot pump, Drake came over and laid a large canvas bag beside her.

"Things for you," he explained. "Jeopard told me to get them."

Tess stared at the bag, wary of Jeopard's continuing

attempts at kindness. She hated the wistful, eager way her pulse jumped.

She started to open the bag, caught Jeopard watching her with a cool, slit-eyed expression, and changed her mind. Curiosity would make her vulnerable. After all, she'd never have gotten into this mess if she hadn't been curious about an enigmatic stranger who had trouble docking his yacht.

She shoved the bag with her foot and went back to pumping up the air mattresses.

When Drake and Jeopard finished setting everything up she had her own territory on the left side of the cave. Tess arranged a pillow and sleeping bag on her air mattress and sat down.

She watched them fiddle with elite camping gear— powerful lanterns, a small kerosene-powered grill, buckets, pots, skillets, and a dozen other items.

"My apartment isn't this well furnished," Jeopard quipped.

He put his mattress on the opposite side of the cave, fixed a campfire site in the center, then came to her and gestured with one finger. "Up. Test time."

She raged inwardly when she realized what he meant. He led her to the end of her chain, then moved gear around to make certain she couldn't reach it.

"Afraid I'll attack you with a spatula?" she asked grimly.

"Frankly, yes, War Woman."

Drake set a C-B radio on Jeopard's side of the cave and ran a long cable to an antenna outside. "Six P.M. every day," he called.

"I'll be listening."

Tess went back to her side of the cave and sat down. "Exactly how long are we going to be here?"

"As long as it takes. Look at it as a native cultural experience, Pocahontas. Cherokees may have hidden in this cave a hundred and fifty years ago."

"I doubt they had C-B radios."

She touched her voluminous jeans and shirt. They were hot and uncomfortable. "What am I supposed to wear?"

"Anything you want. Go naked. I could use the entertainment."

"Perhaps you can amuse yourself by throwing rocks at small animals or pulling the wings off of insects."

"I think I'll leave you two lovebirds alone," Drake interjected. "I'm not a good referee." He mounted his horse and tipped a hand to his forehead in salute to Jeopard. "And you thought the Russians were tough."

Jeopard glanced drolly at Tess. "I know how Custer felt."

Russians? Tess was intrigued, but refused to ask for an explanation.

A sense of foreboding filled her as Drake rode away, leading the other three horses. When the forest swallowed him up, it was as if he'd never existed. She and Jeopard were alone, and the cave seemed awfully small and quiet.

His back to her, Jeopard knelt by a bag, unzipped it, and rummaged inside.

"What now?" she asked in a weary voice.

"Drake says there's a big creek not far from here." He stood and turned to face her. He carried towels and a bar of soap. He smiled pleasantly. "I'd say we both need a bath."

It wasn't just a creek, it was a natural work of art, with a ten-foot waterfall that bubbled over a granite ledge into a shallow pool.

If she hadn't been so upset, she would have sighed with awe. Tess sat down on a flat boulder by the pool and hugged her knees.

"I have no desire to bathe while you watch," she told Jeopard.

He chained her to a nearby tree. "You spent the better part of a week naked in my bed. There's no reason for you to be modest with me now."

She stared into the shimmering pool while a knot of bittersweet pain grew inside her. "That was different," she murmured. "I wasn't ashamed of loving you then."

He slowly sat down beside her. The air seemed to

crackle with emotion. "You're ashamed now?" he asked in a husky voice.

"Yes."

Tess looked at him. A muscle flexed in his jaw, and his eyes were shadowed, but he looked more regretful than angry. She could have sworn that he was struggling with deep sorrow.

"Take a bath, Tess," he finally said, his voice tired. "I won't try to make love to you, if that's what you're afraid of."

He turned away and stripped off his clothes. Tess watched, strange emotions gnawing at her as he revealed his body without inhibition.

Jeopard took the bar of soap and stepped into the pool, his back to her. "Are you coming in?"

"Is this the only chance I'll have to wash?"

"Yes."

"All right," she said in a defeated tone. Tess removed her clothes and slid into the water, then turned her back and sank down until the water covered her to the shoulders.

She heard Jeopard splash water on himself and wanted to cry at the memory of running her hands over his body, of touching him everywhere, of pleasing him in every way a woman could please a man.

"Why did you want me to fall in love with you?" she asked in a tear-soaked voice. "Was I so easy and foolish that you couldn't resist?"

"It was the other way around. I couldn't resist you."

She shut her eyes. *Stop lying to me, Jeopard.* "But you stole from me."

"And after I turned the diamond over to its rightful owner, I planned to come back to Long Beach and tell you why I'd done it."

"You did it for money. Someone paid you. How much?"

He hesitated for a second. "Twenty thousand dollars to my brother and me. We work together."

She gasped. "Who wanted the diamond that badly?"

She heard sloshing noises. The water undulated around her. Suddenly Jeopard touched her shoulder. Tess jumped.

"The soap," he said brusquely, and let it slip down

her chest. He reached for the chain that drooped into the water just beyond her breasts.

Tess shivered as he carefully arranged the chain over her back.

"It was in the way," he said gruffly.

Trying to control her voice, Tess asked again, "Who wanted the diamond?"

He told her about Olaf Starheim, the Duke of Kara.

"But why would he want to kill me?"

Again Jeopard touched her. She wanted to withdraw, but couldn't make herself do it. He ran his hand back and forth across her shoulders, massaging her.

"You tell me," he murmured. "Tell me, and let's go on with our relationship."

Tess's momentary languor dissolved in anger. She moved away from him and said tautly, "I won't forget what you are and what you really want from me."

"Just the truth."

Tess dropped the soap in the water and buried her face in her hands. "I've told you. You don't believe me. You're hopeless. I don't understand you. I don't really know who you are."

"I'm not sure myself these days," he said bitterly.

"You frighten me. I don't feel safe with you."

"*Tess*. That's the one thing you shouldn't doubt."

"Fine words from a con artist."

His voice was more anguished than angry. "You're awfully arrogant for a jewel thief."

Tess grabbed the soap, twisted around, and threw it at him. He caught it just in time to keep from being hit in the head. Slowly, his eyes taunting her, he smiled.

"I'm definitely keeping the spatula away from you."

If he'd counted the times she spoke to him during the next few days, he doubted they'd have come to more than a dozen. She withdrew into a silent, wary world, doing what he told her to do, asking quietly when she needed something, but otherwise ignoring him.

The one time he saw excitement and pleasure in her eyes was when she opened her canvas bag and found all the books and pamphlets he'd instructed Drake to buy for her at the museum on the Cherokee reservation, which wasn't far from the Nantahala area.

"I thought you'd enjoy them," Jeopard told her.

She clasped a book titled *Myths and Sacred Formulas of the Cherokees* to her chest and drew herself up regally. "What do you want in return?"

He glared at her as if she'd just slapped him, then went outside the cave and stayed until nightfall. Had he lost her entirely? She was so bitter that there wasn't any point in talking to her just then. The knowledge that she found him repulsive tore at his soul.

When he returned she was poring over the book of myths and formulas, and he had the disturbing notion that she was searching for some incantation to do him harm.

Drake came back a week later, bringing supplies, smaller clothes and more books for Tess, and a packet from Kyle.

"He's been researching Kara," Drake explained. "He thought you'd like to see what he found, even though it's nothing exciting."

That night, as Tess stirred a pot of soup over the campfire and a gas lantern cast sharp shadows on the cave's walls, Jeopard opened the packet and began reading photocopies of articles about Kara.

"Kara is only a short flight from Sweden." Tess spoke in a rare break from her habitual silence. "I went there many times on vacation. It's a Scandinavian version of Monaco. Tiny and expensive."

"Lots of ski resorts and casinos, it says here."

"A beautiful little country. It's an island, you know, between Sweden and Denmark. The royal palace is a fairy-tale place on a mountaintop that overlooks the North Sea."

"What I can't understand is how monarchies survive in the modern world."

"The people loved the king and queen. I remember when the king died—I must have been about twelve—I was visiting Grandmother and Grandfather in Stockholm. Grandfather, being a member of the Swedish parliament, went to the funeral as a matter of courtesy. Grandmother and I went with him. I'll never forget the people I met. They were sincerely grief-stricken over the king's death. And they adored the queen."

"Too bad nobody likes the king and queen's nephew. Olaf has apparently been waiting all his adult life for the queen to pop off, so he could take over, and nobody's happy about his claim to the throne."

"So recapturing my diamond will win him some brownie points?"

"It's not your diamond."

"And killing me might win him more?" she continued pertly. "Tell me, if Olaf had approached you for that job, how much would you have charged?"

Jeopard struggled to keep from beating one fist against the cave floor. "I don't kill people for pay. That's the last time I'm going to say it."

"Why *do* you kill people?"

"If they're trying to kill me or someone I'm responsible for protecting. And I'm retired from that line of work. I'm just a plain, ordinary private investigator now."

"Hmmm. I see. My father had no respect for p.i.'s. He said they spend their time peeking through keyholes."

"I'm not quite that disgusting," Jeopard told her drolly. "I peek through keyholes, but only for big corporations and governments. I peek through *important* keyholes."

"And con innocent people out of their possessions."

Jeopard ground his teeth. She was retaliating for all that he'd put her through, and she obviously wasn't afraid of him anymore, or she wouldn't be so cocky. At least that was good.

"What else would you like to know about Kara?" she asked innocently, still stirring the soup.

"Why you wanted to keep one of the more mediocre royal diamonds. Why not steal something worth more?"

She didn't say another word to him.

Tess woke to a strange snuffling sound. She propped herself on one elbow and stared into the moonlight outside the cave's entrance. Leaves and twigs crunched under ponderous feet.

She tugged at her chain. Jeopard could run. She couldn't. Tess made a small, fearful sound.

"Sssh, I'm here," Jeopard whispered in the darkness.

Tess realized that he had slipped across the cave to her. He lay down on his stomach beside her. She caught a glimmer of steel in his hand and realized that he held one of the several guns Drake had supplied.

He pressed a tiny piece of metal into her palm. "Open your padlock."

Surprised, she fumbled with it, but finally got the lock undone. The chain fell in a heap on the air mattress.

"Come here." He put an arm around her and pulled her close to his side, shielding her with his body. Tess clutched his warm, hard waist and realized that he wore nothing but briefs.

The night was muggy, and she'd slipped off her T-shirt, so that she wore only her panties. Fear made her ignore that fact as she pressed herself to him and peered over his shoulder.

A huge, dark shape lumbered into view and stopped at the entrance to the cave.

"Bear!" she whispered.

"I know you are," he whispered back in a voice choked with relief and amusement. "I can feel both of your breasts against my side. Your nipples are hard."

The situation was too unsettling to allow her to think straight. She tweaked his back in playful rebuke. "What if it comes into the cave?"

"Know any Cherokee formulas that basically say, 'Get away from me, you big monster'?"

"No! The Cherokees had a lot of affection and respect for bears!"

"Lovely. Just lovely. Cover your ears."

Tess barely had time to clap her hands over her head before Jeopard fired the pistol. A tremendous reverberation rolled through the cave. The bear bolted into the night.

Her chest heaving, Tess grabbed Jeopard's forearm. "You didn't have to shoot him! Damn your cruelty!"

"I just fired a shot over his head! Lord, Tess, do you think I *like* hurting things?"

She inhaled sharply. "I'm sorry, I just assumed—"

"That I like to kill."

She bent her head to his shoulder. "I'm sorry. Sorry."

He rolled to one side, snatched the chain into his hands and put it back around her neck, then fiercely snapped the padlock into place. He took the key back and started to push himself away.

"Jep. Oh, Jep, I misjudged you this time," she said sadly.

The sound of the nickname sent a shudder through him. "This time," he said raspily. "Just this time, you mean."

His hand brushed across her firm, full breasts as he drew back. He cursed darkly and returned to his own side of the cave.

Later he heard her crying in a way that told him she was doing all she could to stifle the sound.

Nine

When he woke up the next morning she was sitting at the end of her chain as close as she could get to him, watching him solemnly, her hands latched around her updrawn knees. Jeopard caught his breath and lay very still, as if she were a wild animal he might frighten away.

She wore a long, colorful cotton skirt that Drake had picked out in a whimsical moment—it looked like something a pioneer woman might wear, he had mumbled—and a white T-shirt with the tail tied in a knot at her waist. The white shirt made her honey-colored skin look more dramatic; her hair was dark silk against the white background.

She was barefoot, and she dug her toes into the earthen floor as if she were scratching the mountain's back. Except for her hypnotizing silver-blue eyes she could have been an Indian princess dressed for the wrong century. The picture she presented was earthy, serene, and extremely feminine.

"Good morning," she said. "I apologize for hurting your feelings last night."

"Oh." His chest swelled with pleasure and relief at her simple words. The night before, her crying had upset him more than her accusations. "I didn't know I had feelings to hurt until I met you," he offered gruffly.

She tilted her head in bewilderment.

"Never mind," he said quickly. "What I mean is, apology accepted. Are you all right? I heard you crying."

"Yes. Fine, the, um, the bear upset me."

Sure, the bear was the big problem. Jeopard couldn't resist. "The bare what?"

She looked at him with guarded amusement. "The bare man who flopped onto my mattress carrying a gun."

"I like to be ready for action when I meet a bear."

"A bare what?"

"A bare woman who snuggles close to me for protection."

This conversation was not helping him get out of the sleeping bag. Jeopard idly glanced down at himself, checking to make certain he was covered. He slept with the bag unzipped and sometimes threw the top back when he got warm.

He woke up hard and aching for her every morning, but since he usually woke before she did, he was able to keep his passion from complicating matters. Just then it would have been impossible to hide it.

"I'd like to go into the woods and look for wild roots," she said politely. "Will you take me?"

Jeopard choked back a pained laugh. She could stay right there and find what she wanted. "Sure. What kind of wild roots?"

"I've been reading a book on herbs the Cherokees used. Since we don't have much else to do, I thought we could go on a field trip."

She paused, lifted a hand to caress the medallion and amulet she had taken to wearing all the time, and added, "But I'd like to visit the creek first. It's an old ritual, to 'go to water' every morning. The Cherokees did it for spiritual reasons."

Jeopard gazed at her with bemused admiration. "You're becoming an Indian."

"Yes." She touched the thick silver chain around her neck and looked a little downcast. "I even feel oppressed now."

That remark stayed with him, making him feel terrible. He moved back on the creek bank, holding the end of the chain but trying to let her have some privacy. There was something reverent about the way she stood in the creek watching the sun rise over the distant mountains.

She had her skirt tucked up to her thighs; regardless of what her ritual meant, Jeopard wouldn't have minded standing there every day at dawn watching the water touch her. He envied it that intimacy.

She bent and scooped water into her hands. "There were a number of ceremonies connected to the rivers and creeks," she called over her shoulder. "The basic idea is that the water cleans your spirit."

Jeopard wondered why she felt the need for it that morning. Was she trying to say that she felt guilty for thinking so badly of him?

"Maybe I should go stand under the waterfall," he called back.

She nodded. "Maybe we both should."

"Come on! Let's do it!"

She looked at him in astonishment, then smiled for the first time since he'd kidnapped her. "All right!"

Jeopard made his way along the bank while she waded up the creek. When they neared the waterfall and its pool she stopped just out of the reach of the spray, shivering.

"It's cold enough to make a person feel *very* virtuous," she said between chattering teeth.

"Good. I need that."

Jeopard wore only shorts and hiking shoes. He climbed onto a rock by the pool, kicked off the shoes, and began tugging at his shorts. She looked up at him wide-eyed.

"Maybe you want to wear wet clothes all morning, but I don't," he explained, squinting at her innocently.

"This wasn't what I had in mind."

"Squaw got no guts."

"Hmmmph." She pulled her shirt over her head, revealing a bra so flimsy, it was transparent.

Jeopard did a double-take. "I've never seen that before."

"Drake brought it. I told him that I needed a spare."

"I'd like to have seen the saleswoman's face when

seven feet of Drake Lancaster walked into the lingerie department."

"I think Drake has a romantic side."

"No. He's not comfortable around women. They're intimidated by his size and the fact that he's such a loner. It's a shame, because he's a good man."

"Any man who picks out lingerie like this is more comfortable around women than you think."

Tess removed the bra and held it in her hand. It was obvious to Jeopard that she intended to look at the bra and not at him, now that he was naked and she was bare from the waist up.

She has the right idea, he thought as he felt a tightening low in his belly. Carrying the end of her chain as usual, Jeopard quickly stepped under the waterfall and stood with his back to her. He could feel his skin shrinking from the frigid shower.

"Virtue!" he shouted in a strangled voice. "Give me virtue!"

A few seconds later she crept under the fall and stood beside him. He looked at her through the veil of water pouring over their heads. She'd removed the rest of her clothes.

She had her eyes shut and her arms crossed over her chest. She shivered violently and hugged herself, then opened her eyes and gave him a watery smile.

Progress, he thought. She was freezing, but she was warming up.

A streak of light slipped through the water, turning it into a shower of pearls. They stood there gazing at the magical sight, then looked at each other.

His heart pounding, Jeopard held out his arms. Sorrow and frustration filled her eyes. She nodded toward the end of her chain, which he still held in one hand.

He dropped it. It disappeared into the water around their legs. She looked as if she were bound to the waterfall and the mountain.

In a way, she was. Her Cherokee ancestors had been part of this land for centuries.

Jeopard groaned inwardly. If she'd let him, he'd cherish that heritage and become part of her life. He continued to hold his hands out to her.

She pointed to the loop around her neck. "Promise me that you'll take this off when we get back to the cave. And you'll believe what I've told you about the blue diamond."

After a tormented moment, Jeopard lowered his arms to his side and shook his head wearily. She pressed her hand over her mouth in distress.

With quick, angry movements she pulled the chain out of the pool and gave the end to him. She left him standing under the beautiful water alone, and went to dress.

Tess dimly remembered some rules about decorum and elegance; rules she'd learned at boarding school in England. They belonged to another life, one she didn't miss.

She loved the feel of the dark, damp earth under her knees and hands as she knelt on the forest floor, digging into it with a large spoon. She almost forgot that Jeopard sat at the other end of the chain, watching her with a troubled expression.

She almost forgot that she'd wanted to throw herself into his arms at the waterfall this morning; that she'd been tempted to say that nothing mattered but taking him into her heart and her body again. What was she becoming, a chained pet devoted to her master and ready to do whatever he wanted? *No.*

"Got it," she said excitedly, and held up a dirty root for Jeopard's perusal.

"Oink," he replied.

"A little respect, please. This is ginseng, *atalikuli*, which means, 'It climbs the mountain.' "

"Or 'It needs plastic surgery.' That's pretty obscene-looking."

"Medicine isn't pretty. This is good for headaches, cramps, and, ahem, female troubles, the book says."

She tossed it into a bucket, where she'd already collected a variety of roots, leaves, and bark.

"It's getting late," Jeopard noted. He glanced at his wristwatch. "Let's start back to the cave. I have to turn on the C-B."

He listened every evening from 6:00 P.M. until ten after. If Drake had any news to report, he'd do it then. And if Jeopard needed to tell him anything, he knew that Drake would be beside his radio at that time.

Jeopard held the end of her chain in one hand and took the bucket in the other. Tess looped the excess over her arm and headed off in front of him, too proud to trail behind or even walk beside him.

He jerked lightly on the chain. "Heel, Queenie, heel."

Her face flaming, she slowed down so that he could walk beside her.

"Smile, Tess, and talk to me." When there was no response, he sighed. "All right, don't. Ignore me. I'll talk to myself." He began a running conversation as they went along, and fifteen minutes later he was still at it.

"Look, a hawk. God, he's beautiful. Have you ever seen a prettier meadow than this? Look, a purple wild flower. *Runamucka.* That means, 'Grows wherever the heck it wants.' "

"Be quiet," she ordered, but she bit her lip to keep from smiling.

They passed through the meadow and entered a lush glade. "Trees," he continued grandly.

She pointed. "I believe that's a maidenhair fern growing in that log over there. *Kaga skutagi,*" she added primly. "It means, 'Crow shin'."

"I didn't know that crows had shins."

"It's good for rheumatism and chills, I think."

"Do you want just the plant, your highness, or should I bring the whole log?"

"The plant alone will do."

He tucked her chain into the waistband of his shorts, put the bucket down, and went to the log. Tess watched with grim amusement as he jerked at the fern without result, whacked the log with his fist, and announced, "I need a blowtorch and a crane."

He thumped the log again. Suddenly a half-dozen red wasps swarmed out of a crumbling hole in the log's side and dive-bombed him. Jeopard didn't make a sound, but he backed up rapidly, with his hands in the air.

Tess ran to him and shooed at the wasps that had followed his retreat. He stood still, his hands still in the air, his face grim and pale. He was trembling.

Tess stared at him in wonder. Had she finally found the one thing that unnerved the Iceman, as Drake sometimes called him?

"You didn't get stung, did you?" she asked in bewilderment, and peered at his bare torso. He'd gone shirtless all day. "Ouch, they got you in three places. This arm, your shoulder, and the back of your hand. Mmmm, I have some rabbit tobacco in the bucket. I'll put it on the welts. You'll be good as new."

"Rabbit tobacco," he said ruefully, and lowered his hands. He took a deep breath, tossed the end of her chain onto the ground, and shook his head. "We have to get back to the cave."

Tess already had a wad of leaves in one hand. She stared at him anxiously. "What's wrong? They're just wasp stings."

"Whatever Cherokee curse you put on me, it worked. All your wishes have come true. You're going to be free of me."

"Jeopard, what are you talking about?"

He looked at her with quiet resignation. "I'm about to have a severe allergic reaction."

By the time they got to the cave his entire upper body was swelling and turning red. He had a chance of surviving only because he'd undergone a complete series of antivenom shots in the past and regularly took boosters to keep up his resistance.

He explained that one sting wouldn't have hurt him, but three were too much for his system to control. Still, the protective shots gave him a little hope.

But only a little hope.

Tess spoke as calmly as she could. "I'm still going to put rabbit tobacco on your welts. At least it'll pull some of the venom out."

She was so frightened for him that she could barely keep her teeth from chattering. "Jep, stop gesturing

. . . what do you want? Be still, I'll get it after I put this tobacco on you."

Breathing harshly, he sank onto his mattress. "Come here. Close."

Tess grabbed the tobacco from her bucket, spit on it, and began mashing it between her fingers.

"Come here," he demanded, wheezing.

She knelt beside him and almost cried at what was happening to his face and torso. His skin looked as if it had been badly burned by the sun.

"What, Jep, for heaven's sake?"

"The key." He patted the pocket of his shorts. "Get rid of . . ." He panted for breath. "Your chain."

"Not right this minute."

"Listen! Guns, here. Ammo, too. Beside mattress. If I die, wait for Drake to come for you. Pull my body out of the cave and *stay put*."

Horrified, she grabbed his shoulders. "I won't let you die!"

He managed to smile, although his face was now so badly swollen that it was a pathetic effort. "Know some Cherokee . . . magic to save . . . me?"

Tess choked back a sob. "No, but I know how to broadcast an emergency call for help on the radio."

"No!"

She ran to the C-B. "My father loved these things. He taught me all about them."

"No! I don't want anyone to know . . . where you are. Might not be safe. Wait till six. Talk to Drake."

"Shut up. Lie down." She grabbed the microphone.

"Get away from that. Dammit, I'll shoot!"

She looked up and found him pointing a gun at her. No, not at her, at the radio. He could barely sit up now. He leaned heavily on one elbow and had to prop the gun in both hands.

"Jep"—she spoke softly and firmly—"I *am* going to call for help."

The radio made a popping sound and leaped sideways as a bullet crashed into it. Tess fell back, holding the disengaged microphone in her hand.

"No," he answered weakly, "you're not."

He slumped onto the mattress and dropped the gun beside it. Then he shut his eyes and groaned.

Crying with frustration and despair, Tess ran to him and knelt down. "I'll never forgive you for that."

"Save you. Do that . . . good thing. Love . . . you."

"Oh, Jep." She balled her hands into fists and stared down at him in desperate anguish.

The histamines released by the stings were making his blood pressure soar. He had trouble breathing, and he put a horribly swollen hand on the center of his chest.

"Bad," he whispered. "Pain."

Tess jerked the padlock key from his shorts pocket and quickly unfastened the chain around her neck. It dropped to the floor, and she kicked both it and the gun aside without a second glance.

She had to do something fast or he was going to die. *He was going to die for her sake.*

"No!" she said in a guttural tone. Tess ran to the bucket of medicinal plants and searched through it. She'd collected a bark that was supposed to act as a mild stimulant; from what she knew of insect allergies, the medical treatment sometimes included a shot of adrenaline for that purpose.

Tess bit her lip until it bled. She might overdose Jeopard or fail to help him at all, but it was her only hope.

Tess grabbed a double handful of bark and threw it in a cooking pot, then opened a jug and added drinking water to it. She fired up the camp stove and turned both its burners as high as they'd go. While the brew was heating, she hurried back to Jeopard.

He was panting, and his eyes had swollen shut. Tess grasped his face between her hands and kissed him. "I love you, Sundance. Don't you dare die," she cried. "I'll wear your chain the rest of my life! I'll do anything! Just hang on!"

He raised his hand weakly, and she sobbed out loud at the state of it. Tess kissed the angry welt mark, then retrieved the rabbit tobacco from where she'd dropped it on her way to the radio. She plastered his hand with the soggy, crushed leaves, then put the same poultice on his forearm and shoulder.

"Yuck," he managed to say.

"Yuck. Good." She glanced down his body and gasped when she saw that his feet and legs were swelling too. Tess frantically undressed him, and when he lay naked she poured cold water over him.

"Virtue," he murmured, his voice so breathless that she could barely understand him.

"I don't know what else to do. It might be the wrong thing."

Tess went to the stove. The simmering bark had turned the water a dark brown color. She wasn't sure if it was ready, but she couldn't wait any longer—he might lose consciousness, and then she'd never get the liquid down him.

Her hands shaking, Tess poured some of the hot tea into a cup and carried it to him. She sat down and struggled until she had his head and shoulders propped on her leg.

"Drink this, Jep," she urged, holding the cup to his mouth.

He could barely open his lips, and his tongue was badly swollen too. After a few seconds of futile struggling, Tess groaned with defeat. She knelt beside him and took a mouthful of bitter bark tea from the cup.

Holding his jaw with one hand and tilting his head back with the other, she put her mouth on his and dribbled the tea down his throat.

He coughed and tried to turn his head away, but he swallowed. "Good! That's it, Sundance! Anything that tastes this bad has got to work!"

She forced the entire cup of tea down him, one mouthful at a time, then got another cupful and did the same with it.

Tess sat back on her heels and stroked his chest, watching him anxiously. He seemed to be breathing a little more easily. "Better?" she asked.

He nodded weakly. "A little."

She catapulted to her feet. "More tea!"

Cup by cup, he recovered. Tess began to wait for long periods between each new dose, afraid that she'd give him too much. When he could breathe decently and the worst of the swelling was gone, she decided to stop.

Exhausted from fear, she slumped beside him and wiped his perspiring body with a wet cloth. When he didn't move or make a sound, she poked him in the ribs.

"Ouch," he said finally, his eyes shut. "Sleepy."

"Sorry. I have an inclination to worry."

"Love you."

Tears ran down her cheeks. She wiped his swollen, ugly face and whispered, "I love you too."

"Must look like a toad."

"Yes, you do. I love you anyway. In fact, I think I love you more right now than when you look incredibly handsome."

"Strange woman."

"Yes," she whispered, smiling.

"Missed your chance to escape."

"How could I leave a man who shoots C-B radios? Such an ornery creature. I had to stay and see what ridiculous thing you'd do next."

"Not ridiculous."

"Not the sort of thing a coldhearted con artist would do, I suppose." Tess lovingly brushed her fingertips over his forehead.

"Think like the enemy too long, you become like him. Can't help it, unless you turn everything off. Machine . . . doesn't feel. No hurt. But no love, either."

"What enemy, Jep? Tell me."

He sighed deeply. "Worked for a government contractor. Agent."

"CIA?"

"No. Free lance. Group of us. Only top people knew about us. Very covert."

"What kind of work was it?"

"Went after specific people. Terrorists. Spies."

"So you worked outside the law?"

"Yes."

"And sometimes you did things—"

"Things that had to be done. No regrets. World's a better place for it. But it gets to you after a while. World seems so ugly. That's why Kyle and I retired."

"Drake too?"

"Yes."

She rested her head on his good shoulder. "My poor Sundance. I understand so much now."

"Tess? Whatever you tell me . . . about the diamond . . . you can trust me with the truth."

"I know that," she whispered. "I know it better than ever."

"I won't ask anymore."

She kissed his dear, puffy face. "Listen to me. There's no way I can prove what I've already told you, but it's the truth. I knew Royce was a jewel thief, but he'd given it up by the time we became involved. He was a lovely man who cared about people, acted honorably toward his friends, and I don't regret marrying him.

"He wouldn't let me take his name—he wanted to protect me from his past. He never did anything that would harm me, and he certainly didn't give me the blue diamond. My grandparents did, and I have no idea how they really came into possession of it.

"I don't know why anyone would want to take revenge on me. My business is totally legitimate. I've never stolen anything from anyone."

She was silent, watching Jeopard's face. He opened bloodshot eyes and looked at her gently for a long moment. "Okay," he whispered. "We start fresh. Go to water. Feel virtuous. Take care of each other."

"Yes." Nodding, crying a little, she smoothed his hair, then lay down beside him. "Now try to sleep."

"What . . . what are you doing?"

"Just holding your wrist. I want to keep track of your pulse for a little while."

"Blood's full of bark juice. Might sprout leaves."

Chuckling, she placed tiny kisses on his face until he fell into a deep, peaceful sleep.

"Get ready," Drake said over his shoulder. "The cave's at the top of this rise."

Kyle Surprise, one hand wrapped tightly around his saddle horn because his horse was determined to make him a tree ornament, pulled a semiautomatic machine gun from the sling on his back. He wondered ruefully if Jeopard would appreciate his greenhorn efforts to ride this damned rock-headed horse.

Kyle just hoped that his brother was all right. He'd arrived from Florida that day, planning to accompany Drake into the mountains and meet the fascinating woman who'd turned Jeopard into a romantic. Kyle had news that would shock them both.

If he weren't too late. When Drake couldn't get a response during the six-o'clock radio call, Kyle had feared the worst. Now that he knew why Olaf Starheim wanted Tess dead, he worried more.

Jeopard was a stickler for routine. If he'd said he'd be on the radio at six, only a catastrophe would have prevented it. A catastrophe or capture by Olaf's people.

Kyle drew up on his horse's reins as Drake waved him to a stop. They stepped down from the horses and watched the flickering light of a campfire dance on the outer edges of the cave walls.

"I'll go first," Kyle whispered, and in deference to his relationship to Jeopard, Drake moved aside.

Kyle slipped forward with a grace that belied his lanky frame. While Jeopard was put together with compact perfection, Kyle was too long in some places and too short in others.

Still, women told him he was just right in the places that counted, and he was certainly no less athletic than his brother. And no less dangerous, when circumstances demanded it.

He crept to the cave entrance, the lethal little machine gun held in front of him. Listening intently, Kyle heard nothing but the crackling of the fire.

Adrenaline pulsed through him. He dived into the cave, tucked one shoulder and rolled neatly into a crouch, the gun aimed at anything that moved.

Not much did. Jeopard, naked except for a towel covering his groin, lay unconscious on an air mattress beyond the fire. He looked as if someone had scalded him with boiling water.

A beautiful woman with lightly bronzed skin and dark hair stood over him, her feet braced on either side of his body.

She was barefoot, and she resembled some sort of gypsy, in a flowery skirt and clinging white T-shirt. A large gold medallion dangled on a chain over her full breasts. She glared at Kyle with fierce silver-blue eyes.

As she pointed her own machine gun at him, she said in a polite British accent, "I am quite capable of shooting you, if you move one inch."

Kyle stared at her, amazed.

So this was the Princess of Kara.

Ten

Tess nearly collapsed from relief when Drake hurried inside the cave and ended the confrontation. She explained what had happened to Jeopard and that he was all right, just sound asleep. She'd heard noises outside and had risen to defend him.

As Jeopard stirred groggily and propped himself up on one elbow, Kyle ran to him and knelt by his side. Tess stepped back to give them privacy, and her heart wrenched at the sight of Kyle's ravaged face. What neighbor's dog was capable of this? She knew that there must be more to the story than Jeopard had told her.

What had surely once been handsome was now a patchwork horror outlined by jagged red scars down his cheeks and across the bridge of his battered nose. Scars fronted both of his ears and made pathways through the reddish-blond hair at his temples.

But his eyes, dark blue eyes like Jeopard's, were so loving and kind that after a moment she noticed nothing but them.

"Damn, you look like an overcooked lobster," Kyle said hoarsely. Then he leaned forward and kissed the top of Jeopard's head.

Jeopard grasped his brother's shoulder affectionately. "I never thought I'd be so happy to hear your insults."

Kyle lifted the gold chain Tess had slipped around Jeopard's neck while he slept. He gazed drolly at the antler amulet, then nodded over his shoulder to Drake. "This is the man who refused to be seen with you and me that time in Brazil."

"Yeah," Drake grumbled. "Didn't like our earrings."

"Simple rhinestone hearts worn on one side only," Kyle continued, "and we *had* to wear them so Alvarez's people could find us. But would my brother let us live that down? Noooo. And yet now he's wearing deer parts around his neck. Does this strike you as a sudden change in attitude, Drake?"

"Strikes me," Drake said, nodding.

"Very funny," Jeopard muttered.

"It's been in my family for quite some time," Tess explained. "I believe the Cherokee symbols on it have something to do with my great-great-grandmother's tribal clan. The Blue clan."

Jeopard glanced down at it, then up at her. She blushed, wondering how much she'd embarrassed him with her whimsy. He looked back at his brother.

"It's for spiritual protection," he explained seriously. "I wear it all the time."

Tess thought her chest would burst with adoration.

"Oh." Kyle looked flabbergasted. He put the amulet down carefully.

Jeopard chuckled. "Nice of you to drop by the neighborhood, bro."

Kyle recovered his cockiness, grinned, and gestured toward the towel that was Jeopard's only covering. "Wearing loincloths these days?"

"It's not kind to make fun of lobsters."

Drake, who'd been examining the blasted radio, came over for a closer look at the angry welts on Jeopard's body. "What kept you from going into shock?"

"Tess saved my life." He explained about the bark tea. When Kyle and Drake looked at her in astonishment and admiration, she bowed grandly.

"Tess, what are you doing all the way over there?" Jeopard demanded.

"I'm standing right next to you."

"Too far."

He reached out and took her hand. Tess sat down on

the mattress beside him. She felt Kyle staring at her and met his stunned, curious gaze with a bemused one. Understatement was the best avenue.

"Would you like some tea?" She swiveled her head toward Drake. "Tea?"

"It'll put leaves on your trunk," Jeopard interjected.

"Ordinary tea for the guests," she corrected, smiling. "More awful bark tea for you, my dear. And you need to eat something, too, now that you're awake. Is anyone else hungry?"

"Got any crumpets to go with the tea?" Drake asked.

"Do you have two spare bedrooms?" Kyle added. "We'd like to stay the night and catch a taxi home tomorrow."

Jeopard made a huffing sound of disgust. "Couple of wise guys, eh? Just for that, we won't get out the fine china."

Kyle's eyes became somber as he studied the two of them. "You both look exhausted. I'll do the cooking." He glanced at their camp stove, and one dark blond brow arched mischievously. "Golly. Just like my days in the Boy Scouts."

"Have you learned anything new about Tess's situation?" Jeopard asked.

"Nothing important. It can wait. We have to get some food into that bizarre-looking body of yours."

Tess noticed Jeopard's frown and the sharp scrutiny he gave his younger brother, who seemed adept at ignoring him.

Kyle vaulted to his feet and clapped his hands together. "Somebody get the melted butter and the lemon juice! I'm cooking a lobster dinner!"

She woke Jeopard during the night to give him more tea. On the opposite side of the cave Kyle and Drake had bedded down with their heads on her air mattress. She saw Kyle raise himself up and watch as she moved quietly about in the light from the camp stove.

"Is he all right?" Kyle asked anxiously.

"He's fine," Jeopard answered.

Kyle chuckled. "Grumpy."

"Nosy."

"Sleepy," Drake said. "Me and the other four dwarfs would appreciate some quiet."

"Go hi your ho."

Tess enjoyed the soft mingling of male laughter that followed. "If this means that I'm Sleeping Beauty, forget it," she told them.

"Because she got poisoned by the evil queen?" Drake asked.

"Because she had to clean up after seven disgusting little dwarfs," Jeopard retorted.

"I think Tess is more the Cinderella type," Kyle interjected.

"Why?" she asked.

"Hmmm." He yawned loudly. "G'night again."

Tess shrugged off his odd remark and finished taking care of Jeopard. After he forced himself to swallow the last drop of bitter tea, she turned off the stove and sat close beside him in the darkness. Tess fiddled with the sleeping bag, pulling it a little higher on his bare chest and smoothing it neatly under his arms.

He raised a hand, caught her hair, and gently pulled her down so that he could murmur in her ear, "I love the way you tuck. You can tuck me all night."

Desire whipped through her, even as she bit her lip to keep from laughing. "Is that any way to speak to your doctor?" She reached for a flashlight.

"What are you going to do to me now, doc?"

"Nothing painful. Shut your eyes."

She turned on the light and studied his face.

"You're not a lobster anymore," she whispered. "You're a paleface again." He opened his eyes and squinted at her. She tested the pulse in his neck. "Very nice."

"Stop. I confess, detective," he begged, blinking painfully.

Tess clicked the light off. The soft mountain night closed around them again, shielding them from Kyle and Drake. She bent forward and kissed him on the lips. Jeopard raised his head a little, eager for more. A sweet, aching heaviness grew inside her belly, and she opened her mouth to his tantalizing attention. It seemed like centuries since she'd tasted him and felt the slow, erotic skill of his tongue.

"What do you confess?" she murmured into his ear.

"That I wish we didn't have guests. I'm out of commission, but I'd love to just touch you."

She shivered with emotion. "And I'd love to stroke every inch of you, but I fear that your poor, pained body might not appreciate it."

He nuzzled his mouth against her ear. His lips caressed her, and his voice was gruff with desire. "At least you can sleep beside me. I like to listen to you breathe."

She buried her soft whimper of need against his neck. "Tomorrow night, when we're alone again, I'll take my clothes off and you can listen to me breathe faster."

"Tell me more," he urged, his voice barely audible.

Tess stretched out beside him and murmured the details into his ear, nibbling him occasionally to add emphasis. He shifted with pleasure.

She wanted to curl one leg over his and rub against him while he moved. She wanted to sift through his chest hair with her fingers and follow its path down his torso until she could wrap him in her hand and feel his hard pulse against her palm.

"I'm swollen again," he told her wickedly. "And bark tea won't make it go away."

"Oh, Jep, no more," she whispered weakly. "We're torturing ourselves."

"I know, honey. I'm sorry." The welts on his shoulder and arm made the prospect of holding her impossible, so he drew her hand to the center of his chest and clasped it tightly.

She wound her fingers through his and said in distress, "We have no corner drugstore."

"We have a seven-foot Cupid named Drake Lancaster. The last bag of supplies he brought included some special presents."

"You hid them!"

"I didn't want you to think I was plotting your seduction."

"You were, of course."

"Of course. All I needed to complete it was three mad wasps."

She kissed his cheek. "How noble of you to suffer an allergic reaction just to get me into your bed."

"No trouble. It was worth it."

They nuzzled their faces together companionably. He sighed with contentment. "The worst is over."

Tess shut her eyes and prayed that he was right.

The next morning Jeopard waited impatiently until Tess and Drake went to the creek to fill buckets and pots with water. She'd declared that *someone* in the cave smelled like a spittoon full of rabbit-tobacco juice and therefore needed a bath.

Jeopard knew she was just trying to give him and Kyle time for a private, brotherly powwow.

"What have you found out about Tess?" he asked Kyle as soon as they were alone. Jeopard threw open the sleeping bag and wrapped himself in a big towel, moving gingerly because his welts throbbed and itched.

Kyle brought a large envelope out of a saddlebag and sat down cross-legged beside the mattress. He tossed the envelope to Jeopard and looked intently into his eyes.

"How important is she to you?"

"I love her."

"That's obvious. Does she love you?"

"Yes."

"You've known each other for such a short time."

"We've barely been apart since the day we met. It doesn't have to be rational."

"Those are words I never thought I'd hear from Jeopard Surprise's mouth."

"Oh? Listen to this. I'm going to ask her to marry me."

Jeopard watched closely as his brother's expression turned grim.

Kyle nodded toward the envelope. "Open it."

Jeopard pulled out an old color photograph clipped from *Life* magazine.

"Look at that face. Tell me what you see."

Jeopard frowned at the close-up of a pretty blond

woman wearing a tiara. The caption underneath said simply, "Kara's Popular Monarch—Queen Isabella." He saw aristocratic features and silver-blue eyes.

Tess's eyes.

Recognition slammed into his stomach and took his breath away. Jeopard held the clipping in one hand and covered the lower half of the queen's face with the other.

"She's Tess's mother," Kyle said softly.

Stunned, Jeopard continued to stare at those haunting eyes. He removed his hand and saw other likenesses —a certain tilt to the mouth, a familiar curve in the jaw.

"Hank Gallatin had an affair with the queen," Kyle explained. "They met twenty-eight years ago when the palace hired him to find the diamonds Royce Benedict stole. The irony was that Royce and Hank were pals.

"Hank got the diamonds back without incriminating his friend, but one of Royce's enemies blew the whistle. Royce went to prison, though he never blamed Hank for that. Anyway, Queen Isabella and Hank Gallatin developed a relationship. She was committed to the king by a polite, socially correct marriage with all the right bloodlines. She and the king had no children.

"The king and the country were her duty; apparently Hank Gallatin was her pleasure. We're not talking a casual affair here, Jep. Their relationship began two years before Tess was born and lasted until Gallatin's death."

A sense of foreboding wound around Jeopard's chest. "Where do Karl and Viktoria Kellgren fit into this?"

"Friends of the queen's. She wanted to stay close to Tess, and she knew Gallatin would need help raising her. The Kellgrens loved Tess like their own blood. It was a perfect arrangement."

"What about the blue diamond? Did Benedict steal it too?"

"No. He had nothing to do with it. The Blue Princess was one of the queen's favorites, and she thought it was ordinary enough that no one would question her if she said that she'd lost it. Of course, she didn't lose it at all—she gave it to the Kellgrens to pass along to Tess."

. "But she never acknowledged Tess publicly," Jeopard said with disgust.

"It wasn't because of shame. The Karan people would have welcomed any child of Isabella's, legitimate or not. But Isabella didn't want Tess to lead the kind of regimented, cloistered life she'd had. She was trying to protect her."

Jeopard numbly laid down the magazine clipping. "How'd you learn all of this?"

"From the Kellgrens. I got Brett Sanders from the State Department to convince them that I was on their side; Sanders is an old friend of theirs. They're terrified, Jep. They know now that Olaf won't stop until he eliminates Tess."

Jeopard gave his brother a troubled look. "Even though she's illegitimate, she's the heir to the throne?"

"Yes."

"Can the Kellgrens prove what they told you?"

"Yes. Sanders went over their documentation and said it's indisputable."

Jeopard stared at Queen Isabella's photograph and fought an urge to toss it into the campfire.

"Jep?" Kyle asked gently. "You look pretty damned miserable."

Jeopard raised his gaze dully and said in a gruff, anguished tone, "How can I ask Tess to give up a kingdom?"

She wished that Kyle hadn't quit joking around her and that Drake hadn't whispered an apology for selecting such a racy bra for her. They were treating her differently now, and she didn't want to be different.

She just wanted Jep to stop looking at her with a guarded, fathomless expression, as if he no longer thought it wise to share his feelings with her.

"It'd be best to meet your grandparents—uh, Karl and Viktoria Kellgren, that is—in Kara," Kyle told her. "Our State Department man has already been in touch with the Karan prime minister. To say that you've caused some excitement is an understatement."

Tess paced back and forth, her fingertips pressed to her temples. Even now, an hour after Jeopard had quietly explained her heritage to her, she felt that her head would burst with the enormity of it all.

"Is this the only way?" she asked, and looked at Jeopard wistfully. "To go there and stake my claim?"

He nodded, his eyes shuttered. Oh, she knew that private, neutral look too well, and it made her ache with loneliness.

"Going public is the only way you can protect yourself from Olaf."

"And that's all I need to do? Then I can come back home?"

There was a strained silence in the cave. Drake, leaning against one wall, shifted awkwardly and looked out at the clouds. Kyle stared at the floor. Only Jeopard met her gaze directly.

"Tess, you're heir to one of the oldest and richest monarchies in Europe. The Karan people revered your mother, and they don't want Olaf to be king. They'll probably welcome you with open arms. Think about the life you'll inherit."

He began to list on his fingers. "Two hundred million dollars—and that's just your mother's personal fortune, Tess. She also had an extraordinary collection of jewelry. A royal yacht that sleeps one hundred and fifty people. Homes all over the world, including two palaces in Kara."

Jeopard smiled wearily. "The fastest sports cars in the world. Any car you want, Tess. A whole fleet of Jaguars."

"Oh, my," she said in a weak voice. Tess fingered the gold medallion around her neck and looked down at it numbly. Her voice broke. "I've discovered *two* wonderful heritages."

She raised her head and gave Jeopard a beseeching look. "But I don't know where I belong anymore."

"You can be a Cherokee and a Scandinavian queen at the same time."

Her heart thudded with a strange feeling of dread. "How do you feel about all this?"

He gave her one of his perfect, noncommittal smiles. "I'm happy for you, of course."

Tess stared at him with disbelief. She'd thought they'd put those kinds of deceptive games behind them, but he was shutting her out of his real emotions just as he had before. It hurt her more than she could put into words.

Everything was changing, even Jeopard's feelings for her.

Tess drew herself up proudly. "I'm going to the creek," she announced, her voice shaking. "I need to think."

Jeopard, who was now dressed in shorts and a T-shirt, rose from his mattress. He was still a little weak, but recovering quickly. "I'll go with you."

"No. Since I seem to be something other than a normal human being now, I don't need company."

"Tess, calm down—"

"I really would like to be alone." She felt as if she already were.

"All right," he said slowly, his voice grim.

Tess left him standing there, his emotions closed within a vault that she no longer had the power to open.

He'd caused his own destruction. The aborigine shaman had been right: Jeopard had brought it on himself. And there wasn't a damned thing he could do about it except sit on his side of the campfire and watch with anguish as Tess remained sitting at the cave entrance, where she'd been since supper, staring into the night sky.

Jeopard ground his teeth together. But wasn't he doing the best thing for them both? He couldn't complicate her new life with a commitment to him. She was only twenty-six years old; she was going to have fame and wealth beyond imagination.

How could she tie herself to a private, moody man with a past that would feed the world media's gossip mill? A man who was ready to settle down and have children? A man who wanted nothing more grand than to stay in these mountains alone with her?

Kyle rose from his spot by the fire. "Well, good night," he announced dramatically. "We're going to have a long day tomorrow. Let's leave by dawn. Tonight I'm 'going to water,' myself, Tess. The sound of the creek might make me forget how much I hate camping out."

"Me too," Drake said, and vaulted up. He busied himself grabbing his sleeping bag and a few pieces of gear, just as Kyle was doing. "We'll see you two in the morning. 'Night."

Cupids, Jeopard thought darkly. *Two large, bumbling Cupids.*

"There's no need," he told them. *Can't you apes see what I'm trying to avoid here?* "Stay put."

Tess swiveled her head and tortured Jeopard with her wounded gaze. "Are you uncomfortable in my royal presence?" Before he could say anything else she told Kyle and Drake, "Thank you. And good night."

They hurried out, sensing the upcoming battle like two old war horses, and anxious to get out of harm's way, Jeopard thought ruefully.

Tess rose, went to the lantern that lit the cave, and brusquely turned it off. Star-softened darkness surrounded the campfire like a lover and enhanced its flickering light.

Jeopard's skin tingled with alertness and a sense of anticipation that was blatantly erotic, no matter how much he wanted to ignore it. She walked to the end of his mattress and stood looking down at him.

Then she began to undress.

Given the privacy of the shadows, Jeopard let his mouth drop open. What kind of tactic was this? No. *No.*

"Don't do it, Tess," he warned in a husky voice.

She flung her shirt and shorts on the ground, followed them with her underwear, and stood there defiantly, a mysterious Cherokee war woman outlined in sensual detail by the firelight.

"I want to see if you can make love to me the way you

did that first night on the *Irresistible*," she said in a haughty tone. "Without emotion."

He groaned inwardly. "It wasn't without emotion. I just couldn't let you see how much you affected me."

"You're awfully good at that. I won't have it, you hear? I won't be shut out now as if I'm some strange, rare beast at the zoo. You can't keep me at a distance."

"Yes, I can," he murmured. "I've spent all of my adult life learning how to do that with people."

She knelt on the mattress and crawled slinkily up to him, a ferocious cat on the prowl. "It won't wash, Sundance. Give up. I've got your number. You can't tell me that you want me less, now that I'm royalty."

"We need to back away from each other. There are going to be a lot of changes in your life, a lot of new opportunities . . ."

He gasped as she ran a hand up the inside of his thigh and caressed him through his shorts. "What does that have to do with you and me?" She skimmed her hand over the rock-hard bulge at the apex of his thighs. "Yes, you want me as much as ever. If this is the only way you can show your love for me right now, I'll take it."

Jeopard grasped her wrist with a trembling hand. "Stop."

"I saved your life. You owe me."

He groaned. She had his shorts unzipped now. "That's not fair."

"You force me to play this way, the way you like."

"No. I love your honesty."

"Then give some in return."

She quickly tugged his shorts and briefs down to his thighs and cupped him in both hands. His chest heaving, Jeopard fell back on one elbow and cursed softly.

"This is honest," she murmured hoarsely. "Your body, hard and hot and eager for whatever I do to it. Is this all you're willing to share with the future queen of Kara?"

"Yes," he said in harsh agony.

"So be it." She stripped his clothes off and straddled him, then ran her hands over his chest and stomach with wicked intent. "I shall enjoy ruining your defenses, my fine peasant."

His back arched as she slid herself over him. Her hips moved fluidly while she circled his nipples with her fingernails. "Love me, Jep," she begged. "Love me the way I love you. *Please*."

His defenses broke apart at the sound of her sweet English voice torn by passion and despair. "Tess, I do." He moaned and dragged her down to his chest.

Jeopard kissed her intimately, sucking the tongue she slipped deep into his mouth and gliding his own tongue between her lips. She cried out and slid her arms around his neck, careful even in her wildness not to hurt his swollen shoulder.

Her body shuddered, driving him to the brink and holding him there as she loved him in a slow, breathless rhythm. He grasped her hips and arched upward, knowing that he'd never get enough of her, either in bed or out of it.

She whispered his name, giving herself to a vortex of emotion that defied him to remain aloof. Lost, lost, he thought as he sank his hands into her hair and kissed her face desperately, licking her skin with the tip of his tongue, making gruff, yearning sounds deep in his throat.

Tess surrounded him with an explosion of pleasure that stroked the last bit of restraint from his body and his mind. He was lifted to a level of loving that merged the physical with the spiritual, until all he could do was float in a dimension where her voice was his only connection with reality.

She called him back, her lips on his face, her hands fervently caressing his hair.

"Did I hurt you?" she implored. "Are you all right?"

No, he'd never be all right if he lost her.

He was almost crying, and as much as it horrified him, he couldn't keep his voice from cracking when he said, "Do you want me to go with you to Kara?"

"Yes, *yes*, of course." She made a whimpering sound. "Is *that* what's upset you? I thought perhaps you wanted to get rid of me, that you'd be glad to send me off without you."

"You think I'd stop loving you that easily?"

"No, but you're accustomed to being alone. And we've become so inseparable so quickly. Does it worry you?"

"*No.* You're the best thing that's ever happened to me. But you need to face the fact that your whole perspective on life is about to change. You can have anything or anyone you want."

"I've already got the *anyone.*"

"You may not be free to make that choice."

She speared her fingers into his hair and looked down at him possessively. "Now, you listen to me. Doesn't a princess have special privileges to do what she wants and love who she wants? Certainly! Otherwise, why would anyone take the bloody job?"

Jeopard would have chuckled, but he was afraid it might sound ragged. "I can't imagine," he told her solemnly, and hugged her to him, wishing that their last night in the mountains together would never end.

She absolutely would not cry, because she didn't want to admit to anyone that she was already homesick for those ancient, blue-green Nantahala mountains and that she was terrified of what waited for her outside them.

The same small jet sat on the same runway, ready this time to take her and Jeopard to New York, where they'd board the Concorde for Europe.

Jeopard clasped his brother's hand, then Drake's. Tess handed Drake her medallion.

"I have a favor to ask."

He looked down at her with gentle, curious eyes. "Anything."

"Will you take it to the reservation and see if anyone can translate it?"

"I'll be glad to." He carefully slipped the medallion into a shirt pocket.

Tess blinked hard and fought a lump in her throat. "I intended to do that myself, but I . . . I'll have to put it off."

Jeopard slid a consoling arm around her shoulders,

sensing her distress. "Damn, I haven't got any hankerchiefs."

Tess chuckled hoarsely and kissed his cheek. "Then we'd better leave this instant." She hugged Drake and Kyle, feeling like a sorrowful Dorothy leaving Oz.

She and Jeopard would have to find their way back to this side of the rainbow, somehow.

Eleven

Of course they adored her. Jeopard had never doubted that they would, but he hadn't realized how quickly they'd take over her life. His despair wasn't helped by the knowledge that no one but Tess wanted him in Kara.

He'd never have let the palace officials realize how he gritted his teeth when someone dismissed him as Tess's *Amerikan livvakt*, which in Swedish meant that he was nothing but her bodyguard. Since few of them condescended to speak English around him except when addressing him personally, he could only imagine the less-complimentary titles they bestowed on him.

The prime minister, palace officials, and an elite team of servants devoted all their time to learning more about Tess. They were still in shock over her, and her claim to the throne remained a closely guarded secret while the Kellgrens' documentation was subjected to more scrutiny.

Olaf was out of the country and hadn't yet been told about her arrival. His dark plans to eliminate her were still Tess and Jeopard's secret; Karan officials simply thought that Tess had decided to come forward with her claim.

And the officials were overjoyed. They saw the potential to develop their own version of Britain's Princess Diana, Jeopard suspected. They were determined to protect and promote her.

They sure as hell didn't consider him Prince Charles material.

During the four days since his and Tess's arrival, the palace-protocol officers had let him attend every meeting with her—but only because she had insisted. They'd assigned him a servant's room adjoining her luxurious ten-room apartment in the palace, even though Tess had delicately explained that he'd be staying in her suite.

As soon as the maids confirmed that the princess wasn't kidding—that she shared her bed with the *livvakt*—everyone went into quiet hysterics.

Sanders, the U.S. State Department man, explained that Jeopard was a former government agent and now a self-employed businessman, but wild rumors started anyway.

Karan officials were puzzled to find that he could afford custom-tailored three-piece suits, since they thought of him as a modestly paid security guard. One day when he wore black he overheard the palace maids whispering in frightened tones, "Mafia."

Jeopard sighed. Now they simply pushed him to the sidelines, and when Tess protested he gallantly winked at her as if it were all some silly game that she and he would win eventually. When she wasn't looking he seethed behind his nonchalant facade.

One day he was waiting tensely in a high-backed chair to one side of a conference table in a huge, opulent meeting room. Tess was seated at the head of the enormous table, flanked by the Karan prime minister and his five-member cabinet.

She looked serene and elegant in a white double-breasted dress ornamented by a sapphire broach that had belonged to her mother. But Jeopard knew that the antler amulet was hidden underneath her clothes, and the way she kept glancing at him over her shoulder radiated volumes of anxiety.

Various people got up and made speeches. Since Jeopard didn't understand Swedish, he had no idea what those speeches concerned.

But he knew that Tess was upset. When it was time for her to respond she stood up and clutched the edge of the table, her knuckles white. She spoke at length in fluent Swedish, her demeanor gracious but firm, and his heart twisted with bittersweet pride.

Even if she hadn't had one drop of royal blood, she deserved to be queen; they'd never find another woman with such intelligence and innate class.

Whatever she was saying, it knocked them on their Scandinavian ears. Strained looks and nervous finger-tapping shouted the politicians' discomfort.

She finished, gestured to him to accompany her, and they walked out of the meeting hall.

Two young men in colorful uniforms snapped to attention as she and Jeopard exited the cavernous room into a mirrored corridor. Tess smiled at them with a polite, forced smile, her mouth tight.

Jeopard grasped her elbow as much to slow her pace as to provide emotional support. "Practicing my silent stares, I see," he teased in a low, intimate voice. "You're picking up bad habits from me."

"Good habits," she corrected grimly.

They walked down a curving marble staircase. More guards saluted and received her impersonal smile as a reward. "Are we going someplace in particular?" Jeopard inquired pleasantly.

"Back to the privacy of my luxury prison."

"Oh. All right."

After what seemed like miles of walking, they reached the palace's residential wing. A butler leaped ahead of them and grandly opened the huge double doors to her suite.

"*Prinsessa*," he murmured, bowing and pointedly ignoring Jeopard.

"Good afternoon," she told the butler in Swedish.

"Take a hike, penguin," Jeopard added.

The servant shut the doors behind them, closing them into a soothing world of Laura Ashley prints and flowing pastels. Queen Isabella had supervised the decoration of these rooms, and they said a great deal about her gentle and romantic spirit.

Tess went to a tall window and looked down on manicured gardens and magnificent fountains. Jeopard stopped behind her, briefly rested his hands on her tense shoulders, then circled his arms around her. She laid both hands over his and held tightly.

"Tell me," he whispered.

"Do you think my mother was happy here? Grand-mother doesn't . . ." Tess inhaled raggedly. "*Viktoria* doesn't think that she was. Her whole life was con-trolled by her duty to the country and the king. She didn't love the king, but she respected him, and he felt the same way toward her. She apparently loved my father, and the king didn't mind. But she wouldn't give up her crown to be with him."

"Couldn't," Jeopard corrected softly. "She couldn't hurt her people."

"Yes, you're right. I admire that kind of devotion, but—"

"What went on in that meeting just now, Pocahontas?"

She spoke sardonically. "Don't refer to my Indian background in front of anyone here. They think we Injuns do nothing but run around scalping people."

"Talk," he urged, pulling her more tightly against him. "Quit stalling."

"They asked me outright if I want the crown and the responsibility that goes along with it—you know, rep-resenting Kara all over the world, lending my support to charities, acting as a proper figurehead. They want me to do it. They say I was *bred* for it by generations of royalty, all the way back to the Vikings, at least on my mother's side of the lineage.

"Bred for it," she repeated harshly. "As if I were a champion racehorse."

Jeopard felt a swift stab of understanding and sym-pathy. "I suppose they'd like to forget that you're half Cherokee?"

"Yes. And that I was married to a jewel thief."

"And that you're cavorting with your *livvakt*."

Her head drooped. "Yes."

Jeopard pressed his cheek to her hair and shut his eyes. He had to give her a fighting chance to be objective. It was the hardest decision he'd ever made in his life.

"But you'd have the kind of fairy-tale life other people dream about. And knowing you, I expect you'd use your influence to accomplish a lot of good in the world."

She caught a ragged sob in her throat. "Do you want to leave me here? Do you? I know they're treating you horribly despite everything I say to them."

Jeopard quickly twisted her sideways and picked her up. He frowned down into her distraught eyes. "I don't *ever* want to leave you."

"Jep, oh, Jep."

He carried her down a maze of hallways to a large room filled with antiques and fresh-cut flowers. Jeopard placed her in the center of a voluptuous bed bulging with soft pillows and canopied in frothy pastels.

Then he knelt beside her, caressed her face with one hand and began unbuttoning her dress with the other. "Want to see what a good bodyguard can do?" he asked hoarsely.

She gave him a tortured smile and reached for him as if her life depended on his touch. They filled the next hour with soothing words and slow caresses. After he made her forget everything except the demands of his mouth and the feel of his body inside hers, he lay next to her and smoothed a hand back and forth over her dewy breasts.

Her languid, adoring gaze never left his face. "I told them that I wouldn't hide my past or give you up," she murmured.

Jeopard nodded. "I assumed you'd said that. And?"

"They're not happy, but they said I could have time to consider my options." She paused. "I don't have to think about it, but I agreed."

Jeopard kissed her tenderly, though he didn't feel victorious. She'd lived at the palace less than a week; she hadn't begun to comprehend how much power and prestige she'd have if she became queen.

"Jep? Olaf Starheim arrives tomorrow. They want to introduce me to him. My second cousin." She added drolly. "Isn't *that* special?"

Jeopard finally had reason to smile, even though it was the kind of smile that might have frozen a fjord in midsummer. "I look forward to tomorrow."

They wanted to persuade her to take the crown, and they went all out, starting the next morning.

She liked purple irises; when Jeopard strolled out of the bedroom wearing nothing but a sleepy squint, he found several maids and butlers setting a dozen vases full of irises around Tess's suite.

One of the maids saw him, squealed, and dropped her vase. Jeopard stalked back into the bedroom.

"What does *otrolig* mean?" he demanded.

Tess collapsed in the center of the bed, laughing. " 'Incredible.' "

After breakfast a palace aide requested that they come to one of the courtyards. There sat four sleek, shiny Jaguars in assorted colors. The aide handed her four sets of color-coordinated keys, smiled, bowed, and said, "From the royal collection."

"Oh, my," Jeopard said glumly, studying her awestruck face.

Several local designers were waiting for her after lunch with racks of clothes and accessories to suit her every-day needs. Then she met with a renowned Paris coutu-rier to discuss "a few simple gowns for your formal needs, mademoiselle."

What he proposed was a wardrobe worth close to two hundred thousand dollars.

"Not including shoes," she told Jeopard breathlessly.

"No shoes? No sale," he answered, deadpan.

They escaped for an hour to explore the palace gar-dens. She wore a very feminine red suit with a blousy bodice, padded shoulders, and white lapels. Jeopard sank his hands into the pockets of yet another black suit and watched her wistfully gaze into a fountain.

She glanced up, tilted her head to one side as if she were seeing him for the first time, and said huskily, "Well, hello, gorgeous. Do you know that you look mys-terious and dramatic in those black suits?"

He felt as if he'd just been enchanted by a garden elf. "Do you know that you're the most beautiful woman I've ever seen?"

Her eyes glowed with devotion. "We are very much in love with you."

"We?"

She grinned. "The royal 'we.' "

His heart sank. She was enjoying her new status, it was obvious. He couldn't blame her, but he ached to keep her from drifting away from him.

"No one's watching. Go ahead," he urged wickedly. "Enjoy the water."

She looked from him to the fountain, biting her lower lip. "All right."

Tess stripped off her white pumps, then went behind a bush and quickly shucked her panty hose, glancing around with delighted naughtiness. She tossed Jeopard a kiss, climbed over the fountain wall, and stood in knee-deep water.

"Brrrr! Jep, this must have come straight from a glacier!"

But she padded around happily, bending down to scoop water over her hands, holding the water to her nose, and inhaling its scent. "It's so crisp and pure!"

"It's probably Perrier."

They both laughed. Tess flung water in the air and watched the silver droplets fall. "Did I ever tell you about the Cherokee fairies?"

"Is this a bad joke?"

"No. Really. The Cherokees believed in all sorts of spirits. They called the fairies 'Little People.' The Little People were very good-hearted and helpful; they were best known for leading lost hunters back home.

"Then there were the *Nuhnehi*, a race of invisible immortals who looked just like ordinary Cherokees—when they wanted to be seen, that is. They were also good-hearted; sometimes they'd show up and help fight the Cherokees' enemies.

"There were also fairies who lived in the caves and on the mountaintops, and some who lived in the rivers and creeks."

Jeopard peered over the edge of the fountain. "I hope a few followed us here. We can use the help."

"I hope so too."

She delicately flung some water at him, as if christening him. "I'm going to bind you to me forever. This is part of a love charm I read in the book on sacred formulas."

His heart pounded as Tess raised her wet hands to the sky and chanted, "Listen! No one is ever lonely with me. Now he has made the path white for me. It shall never be dreary.

"Let him put his soul in the very center of my soul, never to turn away. Grant that in the midst of women he shall never think of them. I belong to the one clan alone that was alloted to him when the seven clans were established.

"I stand with my face toward the Sun Land. No one is lonely with me." She looked at Jeopard solemnly. "Your soul has come into the very center of my soul, never to turn away. I take your soul."

He gazed at her with a sweet breathlessness inside his chest. "Will you marry me?"

So much for objectivity.

Her hands paused in the air. She stared at him, and time seemed to stop under a sky as blue as the Blue Princess, a sky as eternally beautiful as the look in her eyes.

"Yes, Sundance, I will."

He stepped close to the fountain. She cupped his face in her hands and kissed him, happy tears shining in her eyes. Jeopard ignored the self-rebuke that stabbed at him. He'd enjoy this wonderful moment and let the future take care of itself.

"Ahem. *Prinsessa*, pardon."

They looked up to find a stern protocol officer glaring at them.

"The duke, your cousin, is here to meet you."

Olaf Starheim was perhaps forty years old, short and wispy and very pale, with thinning blond hair and pink cheeks. He wore a gray necktie and a gray suit that made him look even less vibrant.

Tess was shocked to find him so harmless in appearance; then she looked directly into his washed-out blue eyes and saw a sharp slyness that chilled her skin.

This was the man who wanted her dead, though there wasn't any way she could prove it.

With a crowd of officials around them, she could only smile at him and try not to shiver when he smiled back. She wanted Jeopard beside her, but Jeopard had been barred from the room. The look in his eyes had left no doubt that he was frustrated by the exclusion.

"What a remarkable claim." Olaf said softly. "So you say you're the queen's daughter?"

"I *am* Isabella's daughter."

"With such, hmmm, unusual coloring. Your father was an Indian?"

"A nearly full-blooded Cherokee, yes."

"But you grew up in England?"

"In boarding school there."

"And you think someone such as yourself is capable of assuming the queen's duties?"

"Yes, but I may relinquish my claim. I understand that if I did, Parliament could vote to discontinue the monarchy."

"And destroy more than a thousand years' of tradition?"

"It seems to me the best of the tradition died with my mother. Perhaps the world is no longer a place where a few can expect privileges because of their bloodlines."

"You talk nonsense, like an American!"

"I am an American. From the original Americans." She gestured toward the Indian features of her face. "And that heritage is much older than the ruling house of Kara."

He was almost trembling with rage. Tess tried to freeze him with her eyes and hoped that she looked half as deadly as Jeopard could.

Then she turned and walked away.

Tess went to bed with a mournful headache caused by seeing what kind of cousin she had on her mother's side of the family. She made a note to call Georgia and learn whether the lawyer had located Erica and Kat yet.

She needed a dose of good cousins to wipe Olaf from her mind.

Jeopard waited until she was sound asleep, then slipped out of her apartment. He found the palace maid who'd called him "incredible" and thanked her with so much charm that she nearly dissolved inside her uniform.

Then he asked her whether Olaf had an apartment at the palace.

Yes, there were apartments for him and other members of the extended royal family. He was in his suite now—she knew because she'd heard a servant complaining about the duke's demands for liquor. And yes, she could tell him how to find the duke's apartment.

When Jeopard arrived there, he told Olaf's secretary that he had a private message from the *prinsessa*. The secretary ushered him into a sumptuous office, where Olaf sat brooding in a thronelike chair behind a large desk.

When he saw Jeopard his face grew even paler than usual. "My people told me that you'd gone to work for her after finishing my job," he said icily. "She provides benefits I did not, I've heard."

Jeopard stopped at the edge of the desk, pulled a small automatic pistol from one pocket, leaned forward, and pointed it directly at the Duke's forehead.

"I know that you tried to kill her. I can't prove it, but it's true. Listen to this carefully. If she has an accident or develops some sort of suspicious ailment, you're dead. Dead.

"Even if you manage to get rid of me first, I have friends who know everything about you. They'll make sure that the job gets done. Believe me, they can find you anywhere, and it won't matter how much money you have or what royal title you have or how well you try to protect yourself. Understand?"

The duke nodded weakly, perspiration running down his temple. "Such bizarre fears shouldn't worry you, Mr. Surprise," he managed to get out in a faint voice. "I'm sure no one wants to harm you or the *prinsessa*."

"You'll return the Blue Princess diamond to me."

"Now, really, your accusations—"

Jeopard pressed the gun's muzzle between Olaf's eyes. "I want that diamond back. Understand?"

The duke shut his eyes and nodded.

"Good." Jeopard stepped away and slipped the gun into a pocket. "One other thing. Your twenty-thousand-dollar fee. I donated it to charity."

Jeopard went to the door, paused with his hand on the latch, and turned for one last look at the duke, who seemed to be wilting behind the enormous desk.

"Don't come near her again; don't talk to her. Ask your people for details about my reputation. Believe what they tell you."

The duke buried his head in his hands as Jeopard left the room.

It was the most amazing dress. Tess gazed at herself in the mirror. The sleek satin ball gown was meant to look regal, and in truth, it made her feel that way.

The sleeves were long and tight, with puffed shoulders. The V-necked bodice hugged her gracefully to the waist, where it flared into a voluminous and flowing skirt.

One sleeve and half of the bodice were a glossy black; the black ran down the neckline diagonally to her hip, where it disappeared under a wide black-and-white-striped bow. The rest of the dress was a soft, antique-pearl shade of white.

Three maids fussed over her appearance, oohing and aahing, admiring the way the stylist had swept her dark hair into an old-fashioned chignon. They called for the valet, and he entered her dressing room carrying a black, velvet-covered case in both hands.

"What's this?" Tess murmured.

"The prime minister asks that you wear these in honor of your mother."

The valet opened the case and revealed a pearl-and-diamond tiara with a matching bracelet and teardrop-shaped earrings.

Tess trembled as the maids helped her don the exquisite jewelry. Her voice shaky, she asked, "Has Mr. Surprise finished dressing?"

The servants greeted her questions with awkward silence and furtive looks. "He was asked to go ahead of you, Your Highness. The prime minister wished to speak to him in private before the ball began."

Tess whirled around, studying their faces anxiously. "Would you send for him, please? He's supposed to escort me."

"The prime minister intends to do that, Your Highness."

Tess rushed up to Kristian Bjornsen as he entered

the anteroom of her suite. The tall, graying prime minister was a Scandinavian Jimmy Stewart; there didn't seem to be anything harsh about him, but his quiet presence was commanding.

"What's going on here?" she asked firmly.

"Mr. Surprise agrees that it would be best if you experience this event alone," Kristian explained gently. "Tonight you'll meet our most important political and social leaders. Mr. Surprise will be in attendance, but he intends to stay in the background."

Kristian Bjornsen paused, looking solemn. "*Prinsessa*, this evening I'd like to announce who you are."

How could Jeopard do this to her? Tess stood beside the prime minister, her hands clasped loosely in front of her, her head up. The magnificent ballroom simmered with excitement and hushed whispers—rumors had been traveling around Kara's inner circles for two weeks, and now they'd been confirmed.

Queen Isabella had given birth to a daughter, and here she was to meet the country's best and brightest; she was Kara's princess and might one day be its queen.

And all Tess could do was stare numbly into the crowd, tormented, searching the room for the man who'd betrayed her.

She answered questions in a daze; she heard her beauty congratulated and her mother complimented; she was told with which men she should waltz and why each one was important.

It finally dawned on her that most of her partners were single, under forty, and members of royal families. With horror Tess realized that she was being presented with acceptable candidates for a husband.

Had Jeopard known about this too?

At the end of the long evening she dragged herself to Kristian Bjornsen and in a soft, emphatic tone said, "If you do not find Jeopard Surprise and bring him to me this instant I shall do an Indian war whoop and throw hors-d'oeuvre knives at the orchestra."

Astonished, he stared down at her. "Your Highness,

there's only one waltz left for the evening. And we've already scheduled—"

"*Now*, sir. Or the only dance I will do is a war dance."

"We don't want you to be unhappy, Your Highness." He signaled a man and sent him for Jeopard.

Unhappy? Was that a strong enough word? How about miserable? Disappointed? And one waltz with Jeopard wouldn't change the fact that he'd deserted her. Tess went to the center of the ballroom and waited.

The glittering crowd began to part to allow the lone, unfamiliar figure through. People stared at the glorious blond stranger dressed in white tie and formal black tails. His stunning entrance bespoke a natural ruler and a strength of character that made him a royal presence in his own right.

Women fanned themselves fervently; men traded disgruntled looks of envy.

Tess looked Jeopard in the eye and saw exactly what she'd expected—a cool, perfect mask.

"I believe this will be the last dance," she said with unsmiling aloofness. "Could we share it?"

He bowed slightly. "If Your Highness wishes."

He held out one hand. When she touched the palm, she found it damp and cold, much like her own. She knew then that he shared her anguish, but the fact didn't change what he'd done.

Jeopard took her in his arms as the orchestra began a dreamy, majestic waltz. She'd never danced with him before, but they melded with the same inner rhythm that made them so wonderful together in other ways.

No one else danced; the crowd seemed riveted—upset, perhaps, as word spread that the *prinsessa* was dancing with a common bodyguard.

"Why did you make a mockery of everything I feel for you?" she whispered. "Are you so easily turned away by what other people think of us?"

His hand tightened on her waist, and she saw a muscle flex in his jaw.

"I'm giving you the opportunity you deserve. There's no other way I can make you look at what these people are offering you. As long as you're with me, you won't know how you really feel about all of this."

"You think you're so much wiser than I am. I hate your righteous attitude."

"I feel older, but not wiser. It's killing me to let you go."

"Let me go?" She stared at him, while her stomach twisted with dread. "Did you know that tonight they've introduced me to a parade of blueblooded bachelors, each acceptable as the queen's consort? Do you approve of that?"

"Yes."

Tess would have stumbled had he not held her closer. Rage and grief built inside her like a thunderstorm. "You asked me to marry you," she reminded him. "And I agreed."

"I won't hold you to it."

"Did I indicate that I'd ever let you out of it?"

He shut his eyes for a moment, and when he looked at her again they glistened with despair. "I'm letting you out of it. I'm leaving for America tonight."

"No," she said weakly, almost moaning the word.

"You stay here and look at this life without my interference. I'll be waiting, and you'll know where to find me."

She started to speak.

"No, Tess, sssh. No vows, no promises that you'll follow me. You've got to be honest with yourself and decide how you feel about the life you could lead here."

Tears shimmered on her cheeks. "Your cynicism is breaking my heart. I'll never forgive you for doubting me."

He winced. "I'll have to take that chance."

The waltz ended. She swallowed harshly, and dignity was the only thing that saved her from digging her fingers into his coat in an attempt to hold him.

He lowered his head, brushed his lips over hers, then stepped back and bowed. Tess stood, frozen in unspeakable sorrow, as he walked away.

Twelve

Millie Surprise McKay was no lightweight. She may have been small and pretty, with soulful green eyes and chin-length curly hair the color of old gold, but she was, in her husband's adoring words, "a little Tasmanian devil."

She'd mellowed only a bit since becoming the devoted mother of a sturdy baby boy nicknamed Zot because of certain impolite sounds he made.

And now she was standing in Jeopard's office, looking deceptively delicate in a chic blue jump suit, while looking undoubtedly upset. She held a gurgling Zot under one arm; the other arm was held akimbo.

"Kyle called me," she said sternly. "I caught the next plane out of Nashville."

Jeopard gave her a hug, kissed Zot's forehead, and led her to a couch. They sat down, with him slouched and her sitting anxiously on the edge of her seat.

Jeopard smiled at her. "How's Brig? Still cutting the new album? I saw the interview in *People* last week."

"Don't change the subject. You've got to get yourself under control."

"I am under control."

"You're wearing a piece of deer antler around your neck! Kyle told me that you rented a sailboat so that you could sit on it for hours every day and stare at the ocean! What is that stubble doing on your face, and why are you wearing shorts and a T-shirt in the office?

"Jep, unlike the rest of us, you were *born* elegant. To sum this up, right now you look like misery on two legs."

"I'm happy to be miserable," he said sincerely.

"*What?*"

"It's good to have feelings again." He cupped the antler amulet in one hand and rubbed it thoughtfully.

"Oh, Jep, I don't know whether to laugh or cry. I've never seen you this way before."

"I've never been this way before."

She sat Zot on the floor. He curled his lips back like a chimpanzee and made an eeking sound.

"My nephew has potential as a politician," Jeopard observed.

"I read about Tess Gallatin in the paper yesterday."

Jeopard looked at his sister dully. "I saw the article. All the wire services carried it. It was the first official announcement about her."

"It sounds as if she's going to accept the crown. At least, she didn't say that she wasn't. Jep, you've been home for three weeks and she hasn't called you once."

"That's the way I wanted it."

"You are one tough *hombre*. What are you going to do now?"

Jeopard cleared his throat, then got up and went to a window. He stood there, squinting narrowly in the bright Florida sun. "Keep waiting."

"Oh, Jep," Millie said sadly. "For how long?"

He lied. "I don't know." *For the rest of my life.*

People at the Fort Lauderdale marina were beginning to whisper about him, but he didn't care. He knew they thought it strange that he kept renting a sailboat just so he could sit on the aft deck in a lounge chair.

Well, hell. He'd never been whimsical before, and he wanted to practice.

Jeopard stood up, adjusted his sunglasses, and walked to the port railing. He fiddled with the chrome work on a post, polishing it distractedly. The newspaper article from the day before stuck in his mind. He'd read it so many times that he'd memorized it.

Sierdansk, Kara—Officials of the tiny Scandinavian principality of Kara announced today that they have verified the claim of an American woman who says she is the illegitimate daughter of the late Queen Isabella.

Tess Gallatin, a California resident, is the daughter of H. R. Gallatin, author of the well-known Sam Daggett adventure novels. Gallatin, now deceased, was a Cherokee Indian.

"We're delighted that she's come forward," a palace spokesman said. "Everyone who's met her has been thoroughly impressed."

The Karan Parliament issued a resolution officially recognizing Ms. Gallatin's royal titles. As the queen's daughter she becomes Princess of Kara, Duchess of Olnawan, Duchess of Cedmur, and Countess of Arvbrijek.

Speculation is growing that she will succeed her mother as queen. The palace spokesman would not comment, but did confirm that the new princess will be interviewed on national television next week.

Jeopard stopped polishing and stood quietly, all his energy and spirit submerged in missing her. He'd encouraged her to stay there; he'd asked for this; he'd once again fostered his own destruction.

But he'd done it unselfishly, and because he loved her that much was a better man than he'd ever been before. He had no regrets.

The knowledge didn't make his heartache much easier to bear.

"Captain Sundance, you really *must* leave the dock more often," a soft English voice called. "Or does the idea of steering a boat still turn you into a bumbler?"

Jeopard whipped around. Tess stood on the dock, looking like peach sherbet, in a flowing shirtwaist dress and matching pumps. Tears streamed down her face, but she smiled giddily as he ran to the edge of the bow and looked at her.

"Tess!"

Jeopard held out both hands. She took them and leaped gracefully onto the bow. For a moment she and he were too emotional to do more than face each other and share a look of tender greeting. Then she flung her arms around his neck and held him fiercely.

"Oh, Jep, being away from you was a special kind of hell."

He groaned and took her in a deep embrace, then nuzzled his face into her dark hair. "When do you have to go back? I read about the television interview—"

"It's already done," she whispered, her breath warm and fast against his ear. "I taped it yesterday."

"But—"

"I suppose you could say it's my hello-and-good-bye interview."

"What?"

She leaned back in the circle of his arms and gazed lovingly at him, then glanced at the antler amulet dangling on his T-shirt. Smiling, she slipped a hand inside the neck of her dress and drew out the chain bearing her Cherokee medallion.

Now it also bore the Blue Princess, in a delicate setting of gold filigree. "I found this in my room after you'd left," she murmured, touching the diamond with a forefinger. "Thank you. I'll consider it a sort of wedding present."

Jeopard grasped her face between his hands and looked at her in bittersweet agony. "What are you trying to tell me?"

"That I'm here to stay and marry you, of course."

"Tess, don't—"

"I know what I'm giving up in Kara, and I don't care. I only stayed until I'd settled my duties there.

"Jep, listen. Drake finally found someone on the reservation who could decipher the message on my medallion. I honestly believe that my great-great-grandmother wanted to send a message to her family for all the generations to come."

"What does the medallion say?"

"On one side it says, 'Katherine Blue Song, daughter of Jesse and Mary Blue Ssng, sister of Anna, Elizabeth, and Sallie. I left my family's souls at rest in Blue Song land, Gold Ridge, Georgia, 1838.'

"On the other side it says, 'Katherine Gallatin, wife of Justis Gallatin. A bluebird should follow the sun.' "

Tess kissed him gently. "Jep, it's a prophecy, and old Dove Gallatin must have known that when she passed the medallions on to Erica, Kat, and me. I can't wait to find out what their medallions say."

"But how did you interpret yours to mean—"

"I'm the Blue Princess, and you're from the sun land. I'm the last princess, just as Katherine was the last Blue Song. Don't you understand? It all seems to hint that I'm *supposed* to follow the sun, just as my great-great-grandmother did. I'm *supposed* to marry you. I even call you Sundance. Do you think it's all just whimsical coincidence?"

"Whimsical? No," he said hoarsely. "Besides, what's wrong with being whimsical?"

And then he kissed her until they were both laughing breathlessly.

Lying across Jeopard's torso in a hypnotized languor, Tess trailed her fingers through the patterns of damp hair on his chest. Then she touched a hand to her cheek and found a fine, furry imprint there.

"You've marked me. I can't go out to dinner," she teased in a husky tone. "People will know that I've been asleep with my cheek on your naked body."

He raised his head groggily and smiled at her. "Then we won't go out to dinner."

"Can you cook?" she asked, as she had once long ago.

"Does it matter?" he answered as before.

She kissed his stomach. "No. Not at all."

"I'll let you do one thing that isn't devoted entirely to me."

"An unselfish man. I love him dearly." She stroked his chest. "And what is that, sir?"

"You said I should remind you to call the lawyer in Gold Ridge."

"Thank you. But I have a problem."

"Hmmm?"

"You haven't left me with enough energy to punch the buttons on the phone."

"If I help, can you crawl up here and give me a kiss?"

"Oh, yes, I have energy for *that*."

He grasped her under the arms and pulled her to him, then kissed her until she collapsed weakly by his side, chuckling.

"In honor of your efforts, and because I love you so much, I'll punch all the numbers on the phone for you," he informed her.

"Bliss!"

He reached for the phone beside his bed, punched numbers as she dictated them, and handed her the receiver. T. Lucas Brown's booming hello made her jump.

"Ouch," Jeopard whispered, and covered his ears.

"Mr. Brown, this is Tess Gallatin."

"Good Lord, girl, I've been reading about you!"

"I'm coming back to Gold Ridge right away. I need to talk to my cousins and convince them that we should preserve our land. It's very important that you locate them."

"I already have! They're chomping at the bit to meet with you!"

"I have quite a story to tell them."

T. Lucas Brown laughed long and heartily. "They each have quite a story to tell *you!*"

THE EDITOR'S CORNER

I feel envious of you. I wish I could look forward to reading next month's LOVESWEPTs for the first time! How I would love to sit back on a succession of the fine spring days coming up and read these six novels. They are just great and were loads of fun for us here to work on.

Starting off not with a bang but an *explosion,* we have the first novel in *The Pearls of Sharah* trilogy, **LEAH'S STORY,** LOVESWEPT #330, by Fayrene Preston. When Zarah, an old gypsy woman, gave her the wondrous string of creamy pearls, promising that a man with cinnamon-colored hair would enter her life and magic would follow, Leah insisted she didn't believe in such pretty illusions. But when handsome Stephen Tanner appeared that night at the carnival, she saw her destiny in his dark eyes and fiery hair. He found her fascinating, beautiful, an enchantress whose gypsy lips had never known passion until the fire of his kisses made her tremble and their sweetness made her melt. Leah had never fit in anywhere but with the gypsies, and she feared Stephen would abandon her as her parents had. Could he teach her she was worthy of his love, that the magic was in her, not the mysterious pearls? Do remember that this marvelous book is also available in hardcover from Doubleday.

Unforgettable Rylan Quaid and Maggie McSwain, that fantastic couple you met in **RUMOR HAS IT,** get their own love story next month in Tami Hoag's **MAN OF HER DREAMS,** LOVESWEPT #331. When Rylan proposes to Maggie at his sister's wedding, joy and fierce disappointment war in her heart. She has loved him forever, wants him desperately. But could he really be such a clod that he would suggest it was time he settled down, and she might as well be the one he did it with? Maggie has to loosen the reins he holds on his passion, teach Ry that he has love to give—and that she is the one great love of his life. Ry figures he's going to win the darling Maggie by showing he's immune to her sizzling charms. . . . This is a love story as heartwarming as it is hot!

From first to last you'll be breathless with laughter and a tear or two as you revel in Joan Elliott Pickart's **HOLLY'S**
(continued)

HOPE, LOVESWEPT #332. Holly Chambers was so beautiful . . . but she appeared to be dead! Justin Hope, shocked at the sight of bodies lying everywhere, couldn't imagine what disaster had befallen the pretty Wisconsin town or how he could help the lovely woman lying so pale and limp on the grass. When mouth-to-mouth resuscitation turned into a kiss full of yearning and heat, Justin felt his spirits soar. He stayed in town and his relationship with Holly only crackled more and warmed more with each passing day. But he called the world his oyster, while Holly led a safe life in her little hometown. Was love powerful enough to change Justin's dreams and to transform Holly, who had stopped believing in happily-ever-after? The answer is pure delight.

Next, we have the thrilling **FIRE AND ICE,** LOVE-SWEPT #333, from the pen—oops—word processor of talented Patt Bucheister. Lauren McLean may look serene, even ice-princess reserved, but on the inside she is full of fiery passion for John Zachary, her boss, her unrequited love . . . the man who has scarcely noticed her during the two or three years she has worked for him. When John unexpectedly gains custody of his young daughter, it is Lauren to the rescue of the adorable child as well as the beleaguered (and adorable!) father. Starved for ecstasy, Lauren wants John more than her next breath . . . and he is wild about her. But she knows far too much about the pain of losing the people she's become attached to. When John melts the icy barriers that keep Lauren remote, the outpouring of passion's fire will have you turning the pages as if they might scorch your fingers.

There's real truth-in-titling in Barbara Boswell's **SIMPLY IRRESISTIBLE,** LOVESWEPT #334, because it *is* a simply irresistibly marvelous romance. I'm sure you really won't be able to put it down. Surgeon Jason Fletcher, the hospital heartbreaker to whom Barbara has previously introduced you, is a gorgeously virile playboy with no scruples . . . until he steps in to protect Laura Novak from a hotshot young doctor. Suddenly Jason—the man who has always prided himself on not having a possessive bone in his body—feels jealous and protective of Laura. Laura's pulse races with excitement when he claims her, but when a near accident shatters her com-

(continued)

posure and forces long-buried emotions to the surface, grief and fury are transformed into wild passion. Danger lurks for Jason in Laura's surrender though, because she is the first woman he has wanted to keep close. And he grows desperate to keep his distance! Jason has always got what he wanted, but Laura has to make him admit he wishes for love.

We close out our remarkable month with one of the most poignant romances we've published, **MERMAID**, LOVESWEPT #335, by Judy Gill. In my judgment this story ranks right up there with Dorothy Garlock's beautiful **A LOVE FOR ALL TIME**, LOVESWEPT #6. Mark Forsythe knew it was impossible, an illusion—he'd caught a golden-haired mermaid on his fishing line! But Gillian Lockstead was deliciously real, a woman of sweet mystery who filled him with a joy he'd forgotten existed. When Gillian gazed up at her handsome rescuer, she sensed he was a man worth waiting for; when Mark kissed her, she was truly caught—and he was enchanted by the magic in her sea-green eyes. Both had children they were raising alone, both had lost spouses to tragedy. Even at first meeting, however, Gillian and Mark felt an unspoken kinship . . . and a potent desire that produced fireworks, and dreams shared. Gillian wanted Mark's love, but could she trust Mark with the truth and shed her mermaid's costume for the sanctuary of his arms? The answer to that question is so touching, so loving that it will make you feel wonderful for a long time to come.

Do let us hear from you!

Warm regards,

Carolyn Nichols

Carolyn Nichols
Editor
LOVESWEPT
Bantam Books
666 Fifth Avenue
New York, NY 10103